The
Wilderness

Sarah Duguid grew up on a farm in North Lincolnshire and now lives in London. *The Wilderness* is her second novel.

By Sarah Duguid

Look At Me
The Wilderness

The Wilderness

SARAH DUGUID

TINDER
PRESS

First published in Great Britain in 2022 by Tinder Press
An imprint of HEADLINE PUBLISHING GROUP

First published in paperback in 2023 by Tinder Press
An imprint of HEADLINE PUBLISHING GROUP

1

Cataloguing in Publication Data is available from the British Library

Paperback ISBN 978 1 4722 2990 8

Typeset in Sabon by Avon DataSet Ltd, Alcester, Warwickshire

Printed and bound in Great Britain by Clays Ltd, Elcograf S.p.A.

MIX
Paper from
responsible sources
FSC® C104740

Headline's policy is to use papers that are natural, renewable and recyclable
products and made from wood grown in well-managed forests and other
controlled sources. The logging and manufacturing processes are expected to
conform to the environmental regulations of the country of origin.

HEADLINE PUBLISHING GROUP
An Hachette UK Company
Carmelite House
50 Victoria Embankment
London EC4Y 0DZ

www.tinderpress.co.uk
www.headline.co.uk
www.hachette.co.uk

For Nico

open water

ISABELLA, THE ELDER OF THE TWO GIRLS, ROWS THE BOAT. At her feet slumps a brown canvas rucksack containing several half-litre bottles of water, four chocolate bars, two homemade cheese sandwiches wrapped in foil and a Thermos flask filled with instant soup: they needed at least one thing that was hot. The rowing is hard work. Noticing her sister is losing strength, Sasha opens a chocolate bar, breaks it for them to share, but Isabella can't let go of the oars, so instead Sasha feeds it to her in little chunks.

'Is that better?' she asks when the chocolate is finished.

'A little,' replies Isabella.

'More?'

'We need to conserve it.'

Grey water. Grey sky. The horizon is nothing more than a distant, blurry line between all this grey. A small wave unravels; its white foam rolls away into nothing. The endless, gentle rhythm of the sea.

Beneath them – could it be right underneath them? – the

body dances with the current. Isabella can't get the image out of her head: bouncing along the seabed, sending up spurts of sand and shells, twirling in the current, carried by the little whirlpool of energy pushing it onwards. Complete freedom. Isabella wishes it was her, swallowed up by the sea, returning to the comfort of a place she knows rather than being stuck out here shivering, worrying about being punished. How could they have been so stupid?

The grey afternoon inches towards evening. Still rowing, exhausted, the girls spot a bright red helicopter heading towards them. Someone must have seen something. Are they searching for them, a couple of fugitive teenagers, or is it the missing adult playing around beneath them that they want? The helicopter turns towards the girls. Isabella pulls the oars as hard as she can. But then the helicopter turns away and, once again, there's only water. They drift. The mist thickens. They're lost. The helicopter switches on its searchlight. Its beam looks like a cylinder of glass filled with smoke.

'The fog is a punishment from God,' says Isabella. 'We'll never be found now.'

'We're lost,' replies Sasha, beginning to cry. 'And we can't see anything. And no one is looking for us.'

'Stay strong,' snaps Isabella. 'We'll be fine. This is a test and we're going to pass it.'

Isabella knows they'll be fine because this is the place they belong. Every sea otter, dolphin and gannet is a part of this world that is a part of them: each belongs to the

2

other's history. Even though they've witnessed the sea's violence – they know that it takes what it wants without fear of retribution – they also know it won't do that to them. Sasha weeps. Isabella pulls defiantly on the oars. Her hair is misted with damp, cheeks sticky from the salt air. Sasha looks down at her cold feet. They must belong to someone else, because she is at home, sitting by the fire. Her mother has brought her a blanket and a hot chocolate, and is smoothing her forehead with a warm hand. Twilight deepens into night. Isabella pulls the oars into the boat. No point tiring herself out. The sea will do what it wants with them anyway. She rummages underneath the bench, hands a life jacket to Sasha, keeps one for herself. Together, they carefully unfold the boat cover, lay it across the damp floor to make a dry place to sit. They slide down on to it. Backs leaning against the bench, they hold on to one another and surrender. As long as there is no storm, they will gradually drift to shore, because everything washes up eventually.

geraniums

ANNA RUBS AT THE KITCHEN WINDOW WITH HER SLEEVE TO make a porthole in the condensation through which she can look out at her geraniums and hydrangeas. The middle of summer: her garden's best moment. She pours a glass of white wine and turns on the portable radio to wait for the news while she finishes peeling potatoes. Sammy, her grey Persian cat, slips around her ankles like a piece of silk thread.

The chicken is ready to come out of the oven when her phone beeps. A text message. David. He'll be late home. She should eat without him. Irritated, she flips the channel on the radio to a station playing classical music. Notes ascend towards a high trill. She carves the chicken, puts a little of the meat on a plate, then wheels her hostess trolley out from the utility room. She plugs it in, puts David's meal inside to keep warm.

Her two sons and their girlfriends tease her about the hostess trolley. She defends herself – it's very useful – and even though their teasing is not meant nastily, it does upset her. It makes her feel uncool and over-domestic, as if she has nothing better to do with her life than keep other people's meals hot while they get on with the real business of living. More and more, it feels to her that living is something other people do. She'd assumed that the moment her sons left home, the real world would come back to her. She and David would do the things they hadn't done when they were young because they were in such a rush to become adults. But it hadn't happened. Still, she cooked meals, organised the house, worried over menus for lunches and dinners. All the things she'd always done. Often, these days, she feels bored. Even as a mother of small children, she'd never felt bored like this before.

At the small table in the corner of the kitchen, Anna sits alone at a table set for two. Her eyes flicker over the room. Perhaps her sons and their girlfriends are right: she is old-fashioned. The arch-shaped panels of glass set into glossy, cream-coloured kitchen doors. The twisted brass handles haven't been changed in thirty years. The hostess trolley is an ugly old thing – even she can concede that – but still, she likes it. It used to belong to her mother, and after all these years, it hasn't once broken down.

In the sitting room, two floral-printed chintz sofas sit either side of the fire. A neat pile of picture books is stacked on the glass coffee table beside Anna's collection of succulents. The smaller plants, new to her collection, are housed underneath delicate glass domes to protect them while they grow. The largest one is almost three feet tall and stands in a polished brass urn beside the table. Very occasionally, she spritzes them with water. In return for her restraint, a vivid red or orange flower bursts out from one of them every couple of years, usually at night. She finds these rare flowers astonishingly beautiful; it takes real discipline not to flood the plants with water in the hope of more. When David does fling open the front door at nine-thirty, he throws his mac on to the chair in the hall, gives Anna a peck on the cheek, announces that he's starving. He steps out of his polished black shoes and goes directly to the kitchen. Sliding around the tiled floor in socked feet, he fetches his plate from the trolley. From the end of the counter, where the old newspapers are piled up, he grabs the previous weekend's colour supplement to read while he hoovers up the chicken. Plate clean, he dumps it in the sink, goes next door to collapse into the sofa while Anna scans the shelf of CDs. She chooses the soundtrack to *Fiddler on the Roof*, sits beside him, gently removing his feet from the coffee table. He rolls over towards her, his hand landing on hers. He keeps it there. His solid fingers curl around her palm. His hand feels warm and soothing.

'I forgot to mention,' he says. 'There's a dinner on Saturday night for a new client.'

'But we promised Fiona we'd see her play.'

'We can see her another time.'

'It's been planned for ages. I was looking forward to it.'

Anna hesitates. She'd promised Fiona – girlfriend of her

eldest son Matthew – months ago that she'd be at the concert. She doesn't want to let her down, but if she stands her ground, this will become an argument. David's work: the juggernaut that flattens her each and every day. David is about to respond when the phone rings. He answers the call while Anna goes to the kitchen. She opens a cupboard door to put the glasses away, setting off a cascade of old water bottles that fall on her head. They're empty, it doesn't hurt, but it's a shock. She curses David under her breath. Why can he never part with anything, not even old bottles? His wardrobe is full of shoes and shirts he no longer wears. He has files of school essays from forty years back, childhood letters, old birthday cards. She gathers up the bottles and takes them outside, where she dumps them in the recycling bin. Why is everything always such a mess? She turns to go back inside but is halted by the sight of David in the doorway, trembling, tears rolling down his cheeks.

'Anna. Something terrible has happened.'

By three in the morning, there is no point trying to sleep, so instead they order a minicab. At City airport, a janitor is still cleaning the floors, but the check-in desk is open. The assistant cheerily tags their bags, hands them their boarding passes for Inverness. David dabs at his swollen eyes with a tissue. Anna takes the passes, tends to David as if he's a child. Does he have his coat? His phone? Wallet?

On the plane, David barely speaks. Anna suggests he push his chair back, gets some sleep, but he ignores her, so she pulls her scarf around her as a blanket, turns her back on him to rest. Next thing she knows, she's being woken by the attendant. The plane is about to land. Through the window, the single runway is like a sticking plaster of shiny black tarmac between a cold grey sea and damp hills.

A long taxi ride across to the west coast, then a boat. They stand outside on the deck, breathing in clean, cold air, watching the land behind them disappear. Further out to sea, the waves swell and grow. Anna keeps her eyes fixed on the horizon to stop the nausea. David grips the railings. When they dock, a taxi takes them across the island to the next ferry. A much shorter journey this time. It's not long before David sees his father, Michael, at the port, waiting for them beside Peter's vintage Land Rover. It proves too much for him. A boy again, he sobs into his father's shoulder, the wind knocking against the pair of them.

A summer ago, the same Land Rover had fetched them from the same ferry, but that time, Peter had been at the wheel. He took them back to a house full of life. When Peter drove, he could throw the Land Rover around as if it were a tiny sports car, but even though Michael has the same height his son had, he no longer has the solidity. He's thin, with a slight shake, and translucent papery skin that shows up all the liver spots on the backs of his hands. He can't conceal the strain it takes to heave the car out of its parking spot.

As they drive across the moor, the flowering heather

makes a delicate mauve blanket, broken only by pale grey rocks speckled with yellow lichen. Michael tells the story to David and Anna, going over it again carefully as if he still can't make sense of it himself. He and Jerri were staying with Peter, Rachel and the girls. It was the second day. They were due to be there for a week to spend time with their grandchildren. He and Jerri offered to stay with the girls so that Rachel and Peter could have a day out on the mainland – they wanted to go to Glasgow. Rachel had some exhibitions she wanted to see. They'd do some shopping, have dinner, come home.

'That was how the day was supposed to be,' Michael says.

Before they left, the six of them had breakfast together. Rachel wore a dark grey woollen dress tied around the middle with a red silk scarf. Jerri told her how lovely she looked. Rachel and Peter hugged the girls goodbye, told them they'd be home around eleven, not to wait up. The rest of the day was normal. The sun was out. They spent the day by the water. The girls swam. They gathered shells, clambered through the rock pools. Jerri stopped them from going off in their kayaks because she couldn't bear the worry. At five, they fetched wood to make a fire on the beach. They'd cook dinner down there. But then Jerri answered the door to two policemen, and everything stopped.

In the distance, two deer graze. Their heads nod as they chew, antlers punching the air. The green bracken, flowering heather and bright blue sky tell of early summer, but when Anna opens the car window, she feels the bite of winter. She closes it again. The car rattles on. Finally, Michael cranks the wheel to the right and the rest of the world disappears. The granite house rises up in front of them, sitting on its gravel stage, nestled among glades of Scots pine and silver birch. To the front of it, the land slopes gently towards the flat, grey sea. To the back, where David parks, the landscape curves upwards to meet the sky, making the house appear to sit within a basin of air. David's mother Jerri rushes out of the house towards her son. Anna has never seen Jerri like this before: frightened like a wild animal, hair wiry and messy, T-shirt stained. Jerri loops her arm through David's, takes him off for a walk down to the shore, while Anna brings in the cases to take upstairs.

In the hall, the handsome mahogany staircase leads upwards towards three arched windows, then bifurcates, giving two routes to the second floor, where another hall, lined with sets of antlers mounted on small hardwood plaques, leads to the bedrooms. Which order do the rooms come in? She can never remember. She tries the first door, peeks her head around, but is stopped from taking another step by the sight of Jerri and Michael's suitcase. She gently closes the door, tries another, to find behind it a bright room with an antique brass bed and wallpaper handprinted with blue peacocks. She puts their cases by the bed.

On her way back downstairs, she stops in the bathroom to claim a space for her wash things by the sink. It's immaculately clean. Jerri's presence, perhaps. Nothing like the last time she stayed, when every time she took a shower, she had to step her way around bottles of shampoo, tubes of exfoliator, home leg-waxing kits. One afternoon, Anna had spent an hour in the bath absorbed by a teenage beauty book left by the sink. Tips and techniques for pre-teenage girls: how to tweeze eyebrows; the difference between a Hollywood and a Brazilian, the benefits and drawbacks of each explained without restraint; what exfoliation achieves; recipes for detoxifying smoothies, and a discussion on whether they could help get rid of cellulite. There were fifteen pages on cellulite. Surely teenage girls found this advice difficult to reconcile with the long paragraphs that came later on self-confidence, on loving yourself, on being 'who you are'.

Back downstairs, Anna spots the tips of two heads just visible over the high back of a velvet sofa in the sitting room. She gathers herself, moves towards them. Fourteen and fifteen: terrible ages to lose your parents. She has no idea what to say.

The girls are holding hands, staring into space. So clearly Rachel's daughters. They have the same bone structure as their mother, the same hooded eyes: lids hanging heavy, half-covering the cornflower blue of their irises, the same air of melancholy. At the sight of Anna, Sasha begins to sob. Anna hugs her, crouching awkwardly on the floor. Isabella looks fretfully at Anna, as if she doesn't want her there, but can't exactly place the source of her dissatisfaction.

It makes Anna feel like an intruder, and yet all the time, Sasha's clammy hand clasps the back of her neck as if she never wants to let her go.

'Please. Anna. No. No. No.' Jerri rushes into the sitting room. 'They don't want us fussing over them.'

Anna scrambles up from the sofa, retreats towards the kitchen. 'I wasn't. I'm sorry. I didn't realise.' Anna turns to the girls. 'I didn't mean to . . . I just wanted to . . .' Her voice drifts.

'Where is Uncle David?' says Isabella.

'He's coming,' Jerri replies.

'I'm going to find him,' Isabella says, running outside.

It is obvious Jerri has been crying. Anna attempts a comforting touch to her shoulder, but Jerri retreats. 'It's their loss I feel the most,' she says.

'But you've lost a child, Jerri,' says Anna.

'He wasn't a child,' snaps Jerri. She begins folding towels on the kitchen table. Her gold wedding ring bangs against the wood as she works. She keeps her head down, folding and unfolding until the towels make exact squares. 'I'm sorry,' Jerri says after a moment. She sits down, pushing the pile of towels away from her so that they fall apart anyway, returning to the messy heap they were in before.

'Please don't apologise,' says Anna.

'The whole idea of this is so improbable, so impossible to comprehend, so sudden,' Jerri says. She has barely finished the sentence when Sasha comes into the room to ask her grandmother, again, if she's absolutely sure that the news is true.

The next morning, Anna and David find Rachel's mother, Tina, and stepfather, Gregory, knocking at the kitchen window. Their journey has been long. Los Angeles to London, sleeper train to Glasgow, taxi and boat the rest of the way. Tina is tired, jetlagged, emotional. She goes straight upstairs for a shower, leaving the rest of them to sit in silence until Jerri thinks to ask Gregory how Tina is coping.

'I don't think it has sunk in yet,' says Gregory.

The door opens. It's Tina, her head wrapped in a turban of towel, another wrapped around her like a peach-coloured mini-dress.

'There's no hot water. I can't rinse my hair,' she exclaims.

'I'll come up with some hot water from the kettle,' Anna says.

In the kitchen, she boils water, fills a large pan with it, then takes it upstairs to find Tina waiting for her in the bathroom. She sits by the bath, leans her head over the edge of it while Anna crouches beside her. Tina used to be a dancer. She still has the poise, the taut, lean frame, the perfectly straight shoulders. So slender that the muscles of her neck are visible, forming a series of strings that run from her collarbones to her jaw.

'Everything's so old over here,' says Tina.

Anna scoops water from the pan with a cup and pours

it over Tina's hair, using her fingers to make sure she reaches all the shampoo.

'I always thought Rachel would come home one day,' Tina says.

'It must be such a shock,' says Anna, continuing to pour the water over her head until Tina stops, pulls away from her.

'Why did my daughter want to leave us and come here? Why did she want to leave us at all? There's nothing here. Just sea and mist.'

'Peter told me the beach you live on in California is gorgeous.'

'I thought she would come home one day. Buy her own plot, build a house that actually worked by an ocean you could actually swim in.'

Anna keeps scooping up water, pouring it over Tina's hair, rinsing it through until the shampoo is gone.

'All that time I missed with her. All the time I'm going to miss with her. How does a car just flip and go into a tree on an empty road?' Tina turns towards the mirror, uses the corner of the towel to dab at her ears, turns back to Anna. 'How?'

When she's dressed, Tina joins Gregory downstairs in the library among the portraits of ancestors that aren't really ancestors at all, surrounded by history that doesn't belong to Rachel, but was preserved by her because she was given the house on the understanding that she would. The previous owner, a distant Scottish relative she'd never met, died without children, so left it up to her nieces and nephews to decide who the house should go to. No one wanted such a remote, run-down place – you'd spend a fortune renovating it, then never be able to live there – so they'd offered it to Rachel, who took that as a great compliment. She gave up her job as a trainee coffee buyer, moved from California to Scotland, and took out loans with the idea she might turn the house into a business: yoga retreats, fashion shoots, a film location. Repairing the roof took half of her budget, so the rest of the work had to be done on very little money. She polished up the old mosaic fireplaces herself, handwashed all the antique Kilim rugs, avoided a costly bill by dusting the old portraits off rather than sending them away to be professionally restored. Tina thought her daughter insane: first for taking the house, but worse, for tiptoeing around all this history. Surely she should do as she pleased. She was restoring it for them, paying for it all herself, doing all the work. What would the family do? Sue her for taking down some old portraits and shipping them off to the auction house? All these gloomy ancestors haunting them. Who in their right mind would preserve all that?

Tina's long arthritic fingers pull at the pearls resting around the neckline of her cardigan. She quivers with energy, like a greyhound. Her fingers dance nervously between the pearls at her neck, her black silk Alice band and her small pear-shaped diamond earrings. Jerri and Michael wordlessly tend to the fire. Then Jerri leans with

15

her back against the wall, her legs out in front her. She clips her nails, then throws the clippings into the flames. Tina looks disgusted. She drinks her coffee, then follows Anna out of the room.

'I need to get out of the house. I need some air,' she says. 'Can we borrow a car? Go for a drive?'

Neither Gregory nor Tina can drive a manual, so it's Anna who takes the wheel of Jerri and Michael's car. At the port, Tina grows frustrated, because she can't understand anything the ticket man says. In the end, Anna has to lean over, shouting through the window, across Tina, so that they can buy a ticket and drive onto the ferry just before it leaves. As the journey progresses, the rocking of the boat makes Gregory feel sick. He leaves the car to stand outside, holding his face towards the water so it sprays him.

'Gregory doesn't seem to care,' says Tina.

'I think he does,' says Anna. 'He is very quiet, thoughtful.'

'No one can understand how I feel,' Tina says.

The ramp jolts as they disembark. They drive on a single-track road. Patches of brown grass the colour of cocoa sit flat against the hill, reminding Anna of wet hair. They pass the shard of an old castle; tall, rectangular, a broken tooth in the landscape. A little further along, where the road widens, they park. They stand in a row looking out to sea. The air is so cold you could smash it. Shafts of light beam through breaks in the cloud.

'God, I fucking hate this place,' sighs Tina.

16

They head towards the castle, but decide against walking up to inspect it. Too high, too far away. Instead, they take the gentler path along the lower edges of the cliff, admiring the ruin by looking up at it from the beach.

Back in the car, they carry on. Not travelling anywhere in particular, windows open, enjoying the view of the sea, until Tina suddenly yells out for them to stop. She's spotted something.

'Back up,' she says.

Anna reverses a hundred or so metres.

'There. Look. Park up,' says Tina.

Before Anna has turned off the engine, Tina is out of the car and standing underneath a tree. 'This is it. This is the place.'

Two black skid marks on the road curve towards the bank, leading to deep tyre tracks at the base of the tree. A jagged gash in the bark reveals the bright, creamy yellow flesh of fresh wood. Along the crack, small flecks of red paint: the colour of Rachel's car.

'It has to be,' says Tina. She searches for Gregory's hand, dabs at her eyes with her sleeve. 'The violence of it.' She climbs the bank on to the moor, where the heather is flowering, gathers some stems of it, along with wild hyacinths, cottongrass, harebells. She lays the flowers at the base of the tree, then stands back, looks it over, returns to gather more. She goes back and forth, filling in the crack in the tree until it looks as if it's been split open by an explosion of wild flowers.

'That's better,' she says.

In the distance, the gulls circle over the sea. The road is empty. The wind has dropped. Silence. The three of them stand in front of the tree. Then Tina turns towards the car.

'Let's go,' she says. 'I want to go back to the house and take a nap.'

Tina doesn't reappear after her nap but when Anna comes down in the middle of the night for a glass of water, she finds her standing in the dark at the window in the kitchen. 'The stars are wonderful up here,' Tina says. 'It's so quiet. I just made a pot of chamomile tea if you want some.' It's four in the morning. Anna doesn't want tea. She's tired, she wants to go back to bed, but she senses Tina's need for company so accepts the tea, and stays. Tina suggests they go outside together because it's such a still, clear night. She was too scared to go alone, but now that Anna is here, she'd like to admire the whole of the sky. They wrap up in blankets from the sitting room, drag a couple of kitchen chairs out. The sea rolls idly into shore. They listen to the call of birds – an owl, corncrakes, song thrushes. Tina talks about Rachel while Anna listens. They stay like this for an hour, maybe more, until the sun starts to rise and Tina begins yawning – the jetlag has caught up with her. She apologises for abandoning Anna – tells her she was enjoying the chat – but must go to bed, leaving Anna wide awake with nothing to do.

Inside, Anna is reading at the kitchen table when she

hears a knock at the door. An urgent tapping. She opens the door, nervously.

'Brendan,' she says. 'What on earth are you doing here? I had no idea . . .'

'It's incredible up here,' he says. 'Wild.'

'David didn't mention you were coming.'

'I thought I'd never find you. My phone died, and all I had was David's instructions on a scrap of paper. I arrived last night but I missed the boat so I had to sleep in the car by the port then take the first ferry across this morning.'

But Brendan didn't even know Rachel and Peter, thinks Anna as she opens the door wider to let him and his small suitcase inside. He wants a coffee, which he insists on making himself – he doesn't want to be any trouble – then drinks while inspecting the view. As the morning intensifies, sun dapples the kitchen, offering flirtatious little spots of warmth, which seem to work on Brendan because he turns to Anna and says, 'David said it was remote and freezing cold up here, but actually it's utterly charming.'

Perhaps David had been trying to dissuade Brendan from coming because he knew Anna would worry about what Brendan might do. Anna has known Brendan long enough to know that he's unpredictable, a little mad, not to everyone's taste. They met at university, at a student party in a basement flat in Brixton. Brendan started talking to Anna. He was attentive to her, kept offering to fetch her things: ice from the kitchen for her drink, more vodka, a cigarette. He told her she was sexy – and intense, which she sensed wasn't a compliment, coming from him. She wore a black skirt, a red and orange scarf, and he wondered out loud if the strait-laced way she presented herself was actually a foil for something wilder. Anna was embarrassed, told him to change the subject. Then David had joined their conversation. Neither of them knew him, but Anna shifted her gaze towards him because she was glad to have someone to break up Brendan's focus on her. David had a fluent, confident way about him; a little boring, perhaps, but he spoke about his reasons for studying law so earnestly that eventually Anna found him endearing. Brendan might have mocked David if it wasn't for his obvious vulnerability, and for the careful way he made sure to ask Brendan about himself. The three of them made an odd gang but somehow it worked, and carried on working because they all remained friends even though their paths parted dramatically once they graduated. After university, Brendan was far too intolerant of the world to find a normal job, whereas David liked the reassurance of corporate structure. Eventually, Brendan became a teacher at a private sixth form college that called itself progressive: pupils could smoke, wear their own clothes, lessons were optional. Brendan started out enthusiastically – this was the future! – but eventually he became cynical, contemptuous even, of the whole system. The kids were too louche, too easy within their own privilege. They didn't try because they didn't have to. He handed in his notice, went travelling instead, but after years of wandering, picking up work here and there, he felt completely lost. He returned home, moved in with Anna and David. It was Anna who had the idea that he should do a PhD in Anthropology. She thought teaching in a university might suit him. And now here he is, Anna thinks, the anthropology lecturer with an interest in the grieving rituals of remote Amazonian tribes, telling her she needs his help.

'Will you show me the house?' asks Brendan. 'While everyone's still asleep.'

Brendan follows Anna, admiring the panelled hall leading to the south-facing rooms at the front of the house. In the library, the best room in the house, Brendan examines the rows of old books while Anna examines him, the way his hair curls around his neck. He hasn't gone at all grey, his hair still the rich dark brown it always was – does he dye it? – but his skin is beginning to fold at the meeting point between ear and cheek.

Together, they poke through the shelves, sliding books out to take a closer look, opening drawers to peek inside. Brendan doesn't tell her off for snooping as David might have done. Instead, he laughs when she pulls out a packet of condoms from behind a book. Only two left out of five. To whom do they belong?

'Jerri and Michael,' says Brendan, and they both fall about laughing. It's a relief to Anna. She hasn't laughed in days.

'There's a particular style these kind of people have,' Brendan says, walking around the mismatched sofas and armchairs. 'Look at this!' He points to a photograph of a woman standing beside a bull. The bull has a ring through his nose, a rosette attached to his bridle and a benign, pathetic expression. The woman holding his rope looks startled.

'I think they're in love,' says Anna.

'Funny kind of love. The bull looks terrified of her,' says Brendan.

'But there's something about his expression that looks so benign; he's imprisoned and yet he's not tormented,' says Anna.

'He's no fool. It's all going to end with him in the sausage factory, and he knows it.'

Upstairs, Anna shows Brendan the little door up to the attic and the servants' rooms, where, if you stand on tiptoe, you can see the views out over the water through the tiny windows. She shows him where the floorboards in the corner have been discreetly carved with initials and dates; little acts of rebellion, of selfhood, that Brendan admires.

'Let's go and wake David,' Anna says.

But when they get to the room, they discover that David is already awake. 'I thought you were coming tomorrow,' he says to Brendan.

'I would have called,' Brendan replies, 'but my phone ran out and I didn't have a charger. I didn't think you'd mind.'

'I don't mind,' replies David. 'I'm just surprised.'

David takes him downstairs and, as the rest of the household awakes, he introduces Brendan to them. Anna's worries about Brendan's presence are unfounded. Jerri puts her arm around him, tells him how grateful she is for coming all this way for Rachel and Peter.

Over the next few days more and more people turn up. On the day of the funeral, there are hundreds of guests. They come from all over Britain, as well as Rachel's family from California, friends from France, Italy, Australia. Some of them gather in the house beforehand, others go straight to the church. On the day, Anna is late to pick up her boys from the ferry because so many of the guests keep stopping her to ask questions: where should they park? Can they leave their bags at the house? Does she know the number for a taxi service? When she finally makes it out of the house and arrives at the ferry, her two boys – she shouldn't call them boys, really they're men – are already waiting for her. They haven't brought their girlfriends. She'd hoped they wouldn't, but had left it up to them. Both boys all to herself for two nights! Matthew wears a black windbreaker, holds a suitcase on wheels. He appears neat and together, whereas Andrew is sitting on a rusted mooring bollard, brown hair flopping into his face, looking as if he didn't sleep much the previous night. Matthew inherited David's steadiness, followed him into a career in the law, whereas Andrew strained against life, even as a baby. He was the child she always worried about, the one sent home from school for misbehaving, the child who wouldn't get invited back to friends' houses. She always found herself defending him, because she loved him so much and could see the vulnerability in him that others couldn't. But in spite of all his difficulties, somehow he managed. He got a degree, then found a job in a tech company doing something Anna doesn't understand, even though he has explained it to her several times. Something about algorithms, user-driven content, platforms.

They get in the car and drive straight to the church, leaving their bags in the boot. They sit in a pew close to the front, Anna between them. Matthew puts his arm around her shoulders, and she feels herself relax for the first time all week. In front of them, the girls are seated together, between their grandmothers. Isabella to the left, Sasha to the right, her head and shoulders two inches below her sister's. They sit rigidly, wearing the stiff navy-blue coats with brass buttons Anna was sent to buy for them because they possessed no smart clothes.

When the caskets are carried in, the girls barely move. A bamboo coffin for Rachel, with wild flowers spilling down the sides. Peter's has a cloth of Murray tartan draped across it. As the coffins pass the girls, Tina puts her arm around Sasha, while Jerri holds Isabella.

The girls don't go to the wake. They stay in their rooms while everyone else mills about in the downstairs of the house. Brendan builds a campfire on the beach and a group of them, including David, Matthew and Andrew, sit around it, drinking whisky and telling stories. David gets drunk, too drunk, which makes Tina cross. It's disrespectful. What is it with the British and alcohol? Why do they need to drink so damn much? Gregory helps David to his feet, puts an arm around his waist. Brendan takes the other side, Anna walking behind them. They climb the stairs, but David loses his footing. The three of them almost topple, but at the last moment, Brendan grabs the banister, steadies them. Upstairs, they help David on to the bed. Anna pulls off his shoes.

'Where have all the years gone?' David mumbles.

'Just sleep,' says Gregory.

'I'm not even in my own body.'

'You need to sleep, buddy,' says Gregory.

David rolls on to his side and passes out.

A few days after the funeral, when everyone has left, Anna, David and the two sets of grandparents sit around the kitchen table, turning the pages of the will. Anna knows what is coming, because fourteen years ago, she and David agreed to be the legal guardians of the girls. A brief discussion that Anna can barely remember, except to point out that the chance of ending up having to actually care for the girls was so unlikely – odds akin to winning the lottery – there was no point in refusing.

Silently, Anna is hoping for a reprieve. Perhaps Rachel found someone more suitable, someone younger, a god-mother or the parent of one of the girls' friends. In her chest, her heart hammers. The pages keep turning until, finally, Anna sees her signature alongside David's – legal guardians. It hits her with a violence that astonishes her.

David begins to speak. They'll need time to work out some practicalities: schools, living arrangements, packing up the Scottish house, when Tina stops him: 'I'd like to take the girls home. I don't want them here in Scotland. We have space in California. We're by a beach. It's warmer. I want to take the girls home with me.'

Anna exhales. But from the rest of the group: silence.

'Tina isn't being deliberately difficult,' says Gregory. 'It's just that there were always plans that ultimately Rachel would come home, along with Peter and the girls. We had identified a plot for them. The plan was . . .'

'But Rachel did love the islands,' says Michael.

'She missed the sunshine. She said that one day she would come home. She often felt lonely,' says Tina.

Jerri spills her coffee, angrily dabs at the stain with a tissue from her pocket.

'She very much made a home for herself here,' says Michael.

'This is very overwhelming for Tina,' says Gregory. 'This whole thing. It's a lot to take in.'

'For everyone,' snaps Jerri. 'It's overwhelming for everyone.' She turns to address Tina directly. 'But for the girls, their memories, their lives, I don't think it's a good idea that we start splitting things up. I understand it's hard for you, that you're upset, but . . .'

'Upset?' Tina hisses.

Gregory stands up, raises his arms. 'It's important we all stay calm.'

'My granddaughters can't stay here in this place, in this house. The heating's no good, the bathtubs are stained with rust, the floors creak, nothing works, it's cold, these weird gargoyles everywhere. What on earth was she thinking? It's remote, stormy, misty. They don't even go to school. They can't be home-tutored without Rachel. She was committed, but who's going to do that? This cannot be permanent.' Tina breaks down into sobs, buries her face in her hands. 'I want to have them home. I need someone at least to be on my side.'

'We're just trying to work this thing out,' Gregory says. 'No one's on anyone's side.'

'We need a compromise that suits everyone,' says Michael.

'Scotland is not where my granddaughters belong. I'm the next of kin. And *I* can decide. I want to take my little girls home,' says Tina.

Tina leaves the room, followed by Gregory. The back door opens, then slams shut, and they're gone.

'She can't do that,' whispers Jerri.

'Rachel chose the guardians. Anna and David,' says Michael. 'It's in black and white.'

'She could challenge it,' says David.

'Tina can't just take them away,' says Jerri. She is standing, pacing the room. 'What a selfish woman. Why on

27

earth would she do this to everyone? To Rachel? To Peter? To us? To the girls? She barely knew the girls. She wasn't a grandmother. She didn't visit from one year to the next. She's all but a stranger. Rachel and Peter died together. Rachel loved it up here. The girls love it here. They don't want to be dragged away like this.'

'David and I were talking about him retiring,' says Anna, tentatively. 'It would be a lot of work for us. If Tina wants to take them, I have no objection.'

Three shocked faces turn towards her.

'Anna,' hisses David.

Anna is in tears now. 'What about my own life?'

'We don't have a choice,' replies David.

'But there's always a choice.'

'We agreed to it. There's a contract.'

'But you're a lawyer.'

'I can't do that to my brother.'

Anna wants to say: 'But he's dead and I'm not.'

'You two are the right couple,' says Jerri. 'You're stable, solvent, the girls know you both.'

'You're what they need,' says Michael.

'You wouldn't be on your own, Anna,' says Jerri. 'Life will change a little, but you'll be well supported.'

'There's Peter's life insurance,' says Michael.

Anna finds herself hissing at them all: 'We're too old!'

'They're already teenagers. It's only a few years,' says Jerri. 'You'll bring the girls to London. You won't have to stay up here.'

To everyone else, it seems simple, but to Anna, it's as if she's been handed down a death sentence of her own. When Tina comes back from her walk with Gregory, she is calmer. 'We'd like to compromise,' says Gregory. 'We'd like visitation rights. Summers with us in California. Every other Christmas, too.'

'Agreed,' says David.

That night, as Anna lies in bed, she feels the same fierce, panicked hammering within her chest. What of her own life? Her boys are grown and gone. David had begun to talk of retiring. She doesn't want to die doing a pile of laundry. She wants to live, to be alive. She longs to go travelling, to take a train right the way through China or across Australia, or go on a horse safari with David somewhere hot and remote. These are the things she wants to do, not balling socks and washing dishes for the rest of her life.

The next morning, Anna avoids everyone in the kitchen, retreats to the library. Alone, the room's stillness is all hers. The sweet smell of wood smoke. Mist conceals the view over the fields rolling towards the water in the distance. She stands at the window, tries to get lost in the haze outside. Anna must put her own life aside while Rachel is free as a wisp. Is she mocking Anna from wherever she is? Anna presses her hand flat against the cool stone of the wall. 'I mustn't think like this,' she whispers to it. 'I mustn't lose my head.'

* * *

It's agreed that Jerri and Michael will stay on at the house, while Anna and David return to London to make arrangements for the move. In London, Anna feels better. She doesn't even mind the polluted air. She gulps down tinny breaths of it as she walks from the park towards the department store. She feels more human, more alive, among all this activity than she ever could stuck up on that island. Shops, cars, people, buses. The city is an outpouring of human endeavour, a miracle that pulls together so seamlessly all the contradictions of modern life. On the other side of the street, a fight breaks out between a taxi driver and a cyclist. The cyclist thumps the roof of the taxi, yells, then swerves down a side street, vanishing before the taxi driver has the chance to get his window down to yell back. All the driver can do is shout into the air: *you cunt*. The word hits Anna like a punch in the face. The driver shakes his head, winds his window back up, drives on. David says the city feels like an assault after three weeks of such quiet, but it's an assault that Anna needs.

At the shop, Anna deliberates between soft pink or primrose yellow sheets. Do teenage girls even care what colour sheets they sleep on? Do girls these days like pink? Would they loathe her for pink sheets? Feel infantilised, patronised, reduced to a stereotype? In the end, she calls her friend Avery, who tells her to stop worrying so much. Just get the cheapest set. So Anna chooses the yellow. Cheerful, but gender neutral, and a full five pounds cheaper than the pink.

Walking home, Anna tries to envisage the girls in London but can't. Cooped up, imprisoned in what will to them feel like a very small house. They've only ever known wide open, empty spaces: huge horizons, the sea, acres of woodland to roam. Girls can't roam London without a care in the world. Something would happen to them. Men would approach them. They're too naive. They've not been prepared for the world. And if something does happen to them, it will be Anna who is to blame. But worse than that, Anna knows she'll find the relationship difficult. She's spent enough holidays up at the house to witness the way the girls are. They are unconstrained by the usual rules of life. The last time Anna visited she witnessed them disappearing off into the woods for hours, or up to the attic rooms. They would appear at mealtimes, then disappear again. They followed each other around like shadows. Anna observed the way they communicated without talking: a glance could mean their departure from the table, or that the other needed the salt, or the water jug, or didn't like the food. No matter how hard she tried, Anna never managed to decipher it. It made her wish she had a sister – but glad she'd only had sons. If she'd been the girls' mother, she would have wanted to know exactly what they were doing in the woods? Why they couldn't sit still? What was going on inside their heads? And yet Rachel was so patient with it all. She never intruded on this intense female relationship, this great mystery playing out in front of her. She allowed the silent push and pull of feminine communication – like an underwater current – to happen in its own way.

Back at home, Anna pushes the two single beds together to make one large double. David said the girls prefer to share not just a bedroom, but also a bed. Anna tears open the cellophane wrapper, shakes out the new sheet. Her heels on the stripped-back floorboards puncture the silence as she swiftly makes up the bed. She needs the double duvet from the wardrobe, but it's locked. She tries the key. It's stuck. She rattles at it, then yanks it far too hard, bringing the whole thing out of its socket, flinging the key across the room.

When she's finished with the sheets and duvet, she smooths the covers to make them neat and creaseless. She arranges the two blue writing journals David bought for the girls at the end of the bed. Brendan suggested them. He said writing down their feelings would help the girls to 'process'. Anna wasn't so sure he was right. She didn't believe in the redemptive power of self-expression. Pain doesn't just go away because you write it down. But she does as she's told and leaves the notebooks.

She fetches a brush, has a quick sweep around the floor, arranges a vase of fresh sunflowers on the windowsill. Just as she is about to turn around to go downstairs, she spots the photograph on the wall of David with their father Peter. She quickly takes it down. It's her job to help them move forward, not to upset them even more. The lack of a photograph leaves a shadow on the wall, so she searches

32

for a replacement, finds a watercolour of some wild flowers and hangs it instead. Done. Finished.

In the kitchen, Anna makes herself a coffee, opens the doors to let in some air. As she sits down to drink it, she hears an almighty crash, as if the action of her arse hitting the chair has set something off upstairs. She runs up to the guest room to find the vase containing the sunflowers has fallen, leaving water and glass everywhere. She gathers up the mess, fetches a towel from the bathroom to mop the water with, then uses the vacuum cleaner to suck up the remaining shards when her mobile phone buzzes in her pocket. It's David's assistant, Matt, wanting to know why David isn't at work.

'But he is at work,' Anna tells him.

'He's definitely not in the office,' Matt says. 'And he's not answering his phone.'

'Is he in a meeting?'

'No one has seen him. All day. He had mentioned taking some time off, but nothing had been agreed. It would be strange for him to just take off like this.'

She glances up at the clock. Two in the afternoon. She tracks back over the morning. She awoke at seven. David was already drinking coffee in the kitchen. He took two paracetamol tablets. She asked him why. He said he had a headache. She asked why. He didn't reply, but then she noticed the empty whisky bottle by the sink.

'I'm not feeling like myself at the moment,' he'd said.

'You need to stop drinking so much.'

'Stop criticising me,' he'd snapped.

'I'm just worried about you,' she'd replied.

He'd drained his coffee, folded his mac over his arm, forgot to kiss her, then left. If he was going to do something stupid, surely he would have remembered to kiss her goodbye.

'Perhaps he had a meeting outside the office?'

'I have his diary in front of me.'

Silence.

'We're worried about him,' says Matt.

Anna tells Matt she'll find out, call him back. No point telling him that she, too, is worried. She phones Avery, who comes straight over. Avery throws her handbag on the chair in the hall and leads the way back into the kitchen, where she tells Anna she'll make them both a coffee while they work out what to do. Anna feels inert. A missing husband. The words don't bind together. She sits, lets her friend take control, accepts a coffee she doesn't want, then drinks it even though it tastes like poison.

In the end, they decide the most sensible thing is to follow David's route to work. They board the Circle line, direct to Embankment, and wander the labyrinth of underground tunnels as if they might find him there sitting on a bench. Anna remembers he mentioned buying his coffee from a small green kiosk outside the station. There, she uses her phone to show the woman behind the counter a photograph of David. Did she see him this morning? Yes, he's a regular. They talked while she made his coffee, then he left. Did he seem agitated, different?

'He was normal,' says the woman. 'Polite. He chatted a bit.'

They follow his route to the office, then walk back using a different way. Anna phones an old school friend of David's. No, he hasn't heard from him, but he'll ring around. She tries Stephen, whom he went to law school with, but he doesn't answer, so she leaves a message. Avery spots a gap between two buildings, revealing a glimpse of the river, suggests they follow it. They head west past the Savoy, past former gentlemen's clubs, boats turned into bars. Beyond this, where it is quieter, they stop to sit on a bench overlooking the water. A stick floats past them. 'You don't think he would have . . .' says Anna.

'No,' says Avery. 'I don't.'

'When do we call the police?' asks Anna.

'Not yet,' says Avery. 'Not today.'

In the end, Anna dials David's mother, which she hadn't wanted to do.

'Brendan,' says Jerri. 'Do you have Brendan's number? I bet he's there. He's been speaking about him a lot lately.'

Anna tries Brendan. No, he hasn't seen David but he's most likely fine, he's a sensible chap, maybe he just needs some space. Perhaps he's feeling overwhelmed. Either way, he'll be home soon. He's not the type to vanish. 'Stop worrying, Anna. He'll be fine,' Brendan says.

'Tell me where he is,' she replies.

A pause.

'Tell me,' says Anna again.

'David is with me,' Brendan says.

Brendan lives at the very edge of London, just before it turns into countryside. His house is neat and suburban, flanked by neighbours who are not his type at all: lawns mown, cars washed, savings in the bank; polished nick-nacks lined up on their front windowsills. Anna heads up the tarmac drive to his front door, which is housed within a porch made of privacy glass. Unlocked. Anna walks straight in without announcing her arrival. She wants to surprise them, find out exactly what they are doing before they have the chance to hide it.

She passes through the kitchen, with all of its evidence of Brendan's solitary, bachelor's existence: the single coffee mug washed and turned upside down on the empty draining board; a box of instant soup by the kettle; packets of pasta neatly re-closed with the sticky label; socks and underpants drying on a laundry rack. On the tiled sills of the windows that overlook the lawn is Brendan's collection of tribal artefacts: carved swords, painted face masks with grey horsehair beards, penis gourds from Papua New Guinea, old drinking horns. Anna moves slowly towards the sitting room, throws open the door to find David crouched on the floor, a long pipe in his mouth, a colourful tube leading to a glass vase of bubbling water.

'David, what are you doing?'

He looks up. Shocked, like a schoolboy caught out by

his mum. He pauses as if trying to find an explanation, but fails, has no choice but to fall back on the truth. 'I'm smoking a bong,' he says.

'With marijuana in it?'

'Yes,' he replies.

Brendan is sitting cross-legged on a small cushion on the floor, but gets up, heads in Anna's direction. He tries to hug her, but Anna shakes him off.

'I've been out looking for you all day,' she says.

'What would you like?' asks Brendan. 'Cup of tea? Glass of water?'

'David, what are you doing?'

'Having a day off.'

'I didn't know where you were.'

'Anna,' David says. 'Sit down. I need to talk to you. There's been a change of plan. Brendan has been telling me for weeks that he thinks it's a bad idea to bring the girls down to London. He's been saying they need to stay where they are for longer. It's too much for them. I've spoken to my mother and Rachel's mother, and they all agree. It's too soon to uproot them. It's only been three months, and apparently they're not coping at all. They're not sleeping well. Not talking much. My mother says if anything, they're worse rather than better.'

Anna exhales with a sudden flood of relief. She feels herself lighten. They won't be coming. In that instant, she realises how much their arrival has been weighing on her. The dread of sharing her home, the enormous responsibility,

37

the pressure to get along with them. These two girls with no fixed departure date, needing to be fed and entertained, day after day. Having to be a mother again, or a poor imitation of one, just as she's finished with all that.

'I knew you'd be OK about it,' David says.

'We'll have to sort out some kind of help, though, for your parents. They're too old to be running all of that. They'll need some practical help. They'll never cope.'

David turns to face her. 'Anna,' he says. 'You've misunderstood. We're going there. We're going to move in with them. Up there.'

'What?'

'We are very concerned about the girls.'

'We were trying to find our moment to tell you,' says Brendan.

'We?' snaps Anna.

'It was David, David was waiting for the right . . .' Brendan replies.

'I can't just be moved around the country as if I'm an empty suitcase. You can't make decisions like that without even consulting me.'

'Brendan brought up the idea,' says David. 'He didn't like the sound of too much change. The girls are still fragile. Too fragile to have to begin a whole new life, a new school, a new home. My mother has agreed. They need a familiar place. If everything changes, it will be too much for their young psyches.'

'And what about my psyche?' Anna says.

38

'They're not adults. They wouldn't cope. I did look it all up on Google, and Brendan is right. They don't have the same developed sense of identity that we have. It is absolutely the right thing to do. I've talked to the office about a three-month sabbatical. My deputy can handle everything. And after that, if needs be, I might be able to work remotely. Or just give up work.'

'Do we have to do everything Brendan tells us to?'

'I'm going to let you both talk,' says Brendan, leaving the room.

David holds both of Anna's hands. 'We have to get it right, just for these first precious months with those two girls. I have to get it right. I have to. I need to. It's so important.' He pauses. 'I know I'm a shit to live with at the moment, Anna, but it will get better. Things will change.'

'Brendan's not a psychologist – he's an anthropologist, and not a very good one at that. He has no right to claim all this psychological expertise,' whispers Anna, pulling one of her hands away.

'Don't be angry,' says David.

'I'm the legal guardian, too.'

'Brendan is concerned about you as well. We had a long chat about you today. He adores you, Anna.' David reaches for the hand Anna has removed from his clutch. 'We'll go up there, we'll make them better, then when they're ready, we'll bring them home. We can manage that. We both need something different, too. I need something different. Men my age drop dead of heart attacks. Let's help them find their feet again, so they're strong enough to live life again, then we'll bring them back here. It might even be fun.'

Back at home, in the spare bedroom, Anna rips the sheets from each bed. She screws them into a rough heap, stuffs them into the back of the wardrobe. She runs a bath. Mountain ranges of white crackling suds shift across its surface. She uses her toe to form a break in the bubbles, slips into the water.

When she's finished, she changes for bed. The sound of David coming upstairs compels her to put the light out. Pretend to be asleep. In the bathroom, the tap is running, his electric toothbrush, him spitting, then he pulls back the covers, creeps into bed beside her. The smell of fresh mint toothpaste. A cold draught as he ruffles the covers to get comfortable. She rolls over, away from him, but he moves towards her, pressing into her body. His back moulds towards the shape of hers. She wants to move away. This hot line against her makes Anna want to disappear. The oppressive heat of his body as he rolls her over. The weight of him on top of her. He'll crush her. But she lets him anyway, and when he rolls off her, still panting, she feels shot through with self-loathing.

'I hate it when we fight,' he says. 'I'm glad we've made up.'

Later, still unable to sleep, she whispers to him: 'I don't want to go,' but David doesn't reply.

In the dark, she hates him. She hates the sound of his

breath as it upsets the silence of the night. She hates the smell of him, the way the bed dips in his direction. She hates his shoes, his dirty shoes waiting for his clammy feet. She hates the black leather belt dangling from his trousers.

Anna doesn't sleep much. The morning comes as a relief. The sound of birdsong. She feels heavy, devoid of energy, but gets out of bed, drawn by the thought of the silence and solitude downstairs. She pulls the curtain away from the window behind her bed. The sky is clear. A soft, muted blue. The sun washes everything in powdery, morning light.

At the sight of the outdoors, she wonders if she'd worried too much. The light and the morning bring everything back into perspective. It won't be forever. She can survive a few months away from home. She can live in that house. That beautiful, secluded place with the sea at the bottom of the garden. She watches David sleeping. At the window, two cabbage white butterflies, unsteady and fragile, land on leaves. They seem to be squabbling, patting the air away with their wings until one butterfly removes himself to a different leaf and the commotion is over.

Anna sets the pan to boil an egg for breakfast. She fills the toaster with bread. She finds herself hoping David won't come down for at least another half an hour, because she is enjoying the morning without him.

David is still not awake when Anna leaves the house to go to Hyde Park to meet her walking group by the

Serpentine. A long, brisk march around the lake to restore her then up to Kensington Gardens where they usually finish off with a coffee at the outdoor café but this morning, Anna doesn't stay because she's offered to help her friend Avery move house, and she wants to get there early.

On her way to the bus, she sends Avery a text telling her she'll be earlier than planned, and even though she doesn't get a reply, she carries on. Avery won't mind if she just turns up. But when Avery opens her front door, still wearing pyjamas, Anna realises she'd been asleep. She apologises, blurts out that David is being awful – a complete arsehole – which is why she couldn't wait.

'Make us some coffee while I get ready,' replies Avery. 'I won't be long.'

But Anna can't wait, she needs to talk to someone so she follows her friend, aware how needy she's being. Through the bedroom door, she gives Avery the rest of the details of the argument until in the end Avery pops her head around the door, tells Anna she'll be in the shower and won't be able to hear her for a while. Anna retreats to the kitchen, makes the coffee then sits at the table to work through the pages of a news magazine while she waits. Halfway through, she lingers over a series of photographs. It's called Airstrikes, and has been shortlisted for an important journalism award. Children with soft hands and feet covered in grey dust. The same grey dust stopping the flow of blood down their cheeks. A young boy throws an empty shell as if it were a ball. Then a large centre spread makes her stop. An image of a woman lit by bright, phosphorescent sunlight that beams through a gap between two ugly concrete buildings. They've been bombed, they're crumbling, but the way the light falls gives the image a magical, other-worldly beauty. Dust particles twinkle around this woman like glitter as she works her market stall, laid out half with vegetables – green tomatoes, some potatoes, red and orange peppers – and half with cleaning products. Sunshine-yellow washing-up liquid, bars of bright pink soap, scrubbing brushes with vivid blue handles. All these primary colours, like children's sweets among this destruction. Anna keeps looking into this woman's eyes, trying to gauge what she must have felt that day: what was she doing selling cleaning products in the aftermath of an apocalypse? She's still lost in the picture when Avery appears in the sitting room doorway and says: 'You know, you could leave him.'

Anna struggles to get her words out, to respond to this, to tell Avery that yes, she's cross but she and David are, for the most part, fine. Why on earth would she want to leave?

'To have your own life,' says Avery.

This is a shock to Anna. 'But we've been married a very long time. We've laid down a structure around which other people have built their lives. It would be impossible to topple our marriage without bringing down the lives of all the other people around us.'

'But Anna, your kids are twenty-five and twenty-seven.'

'It's not just them.'

She doesn't want to reveal to Avery any more than that. All these pieces of her life, the scaffolding and wires holding David and her together: the people they know; the place they live; the money they spend; the holidays they take. The thought terrifies Anna, shakes her around the edges of herself. Have a life? This is her life.

'All I'm saying, Anna, is that it is not beyond the realms of possibility that a woman whose husband expects her, as she approaches sixty, to just give up her life and raise two girls, might say enough is enough. All that you've done for him, for all of these years. It's not just this. It's everything. All the times you were let down because he stayed at the office. The career you gave up. The dishes you washed. The food you prepared. The house you cleaned. The children's lunches you organised. And now this. His expectations are so extravagantly, extraordinarily selfish that it's not just thoughtless – it's offensive. Offensive to you, as a human being, with a beating heart and the entitlement to live a life.'

Anna doesn't respond. She doesn't know how to. She's worried about David. The diligent, hard-working shipping lawyer, the man who likes routine, the man she doesn't recognise at the moment. Unshaven face, sunken cheeks, drinking whisky until two in the morning, trudging into work with a hangover. As a young man, he slipped without any resistance into a career in law. He chose it. It chose him. He worked at it with singular determination, as if nothing else mattered. At the dinner they had to celebrate

44

his promotion to partner, people came up to her one after another to congratulate her: no one makes partner so young. Anna couldn't understand why they congratulated *her*, but she took the praise, nonetheless. That night she wore a red dress, ate octopus. It was prettily arranged on square plates, a frill of pink and white with dots of a dark green oil and pale pink microherbs. She was barely into her thirties and already she felt so grown up. This life they were making for themselves. She had two children, which despite meaning that she no longer went out to work, gave her a sense of fullness, of purpose. Together, she and David found their own coexistence, a gentle understanding of one another. David provided money; Anna took charge of the house. Old-fashioned, but she hadn't minded that. She'd been surprised by how much she enjoyed the parts of domestic life that others found boring. And now this. *You smell*, she'd had to say to him that morning. *You smell of sweat and alcohol. You can't go into the office like that.*

'Avery, it's difficult to . . .'

'My point is that it's your turn to have a life,' says Avery.

'I'm not ready to hate him.'

'You don't have to.'

'Then I'm not ready to be hated.'

'There's a middle ground.'

'I'm not like you, Avery. I'm not fearless and bold. I can't tell the whole world to fuck off just because I feel like it.'

'The choice isn't between being an angel or a devil,' says

Avery, standing up from her chair. Her lip is quivering. Her cheeks are flushed, but her voice remains calm as they inch towards a conversation that is raw for both of them. Is there not a note of jealousy in Avery's advice? Avery's insistence on her own freedom, on how wonderful it all is, on how all women should join her club. Anna knows not to question it, not to needle Avery into deeper admissions.

'All I'm saying is that a rebellion wouldn't do David any harm at all. Men agree to things knowing the only contribution they'll be making is to provide a wife to do all the hard graft.'

Anna looks at her blankly.

'That's you,' says Avery. 'You'll be doing all the work.'

'I know,' says Anna.

'I shouldn't have said anything,' replies Avery.

'But you're probably right. I just don't want to think about it at the moment.'

Avery holds open a black bin bag. 'Where do we begin?' she asks.

'Chuck all that,' says Anna, pointing to the stained old cookery books Avery never uses, the plaits of dried-out garlic, the ancient, inedible chillies dangling from a dusty string, and empty bottles she plans one day to use as candleholders. 'All of it can go.'

'I must be getting old. Thirty years in one place, then a sudden urge for a garden. It's a sign of old age, isn't it?'

'You are not going far. You'll still be in the city, just a little further out. You'll love it when you get there,' says

Anna. 'Today is one difficult day. When you're in the new place, out in the garden with a group of friends around, all this will be a distant memory.'

It's the first time Avery's moved since Anna has known her. She's lived in this tiny flat on the top floor of an old Georgian house for the past thirty years, ever since Anna and Avery met each other at secretarial college. They shared a typewriter on their first day, politely taking turns on it, then going for a bowl of soup together at the café across the road after lessons. Even though they were opposites in every way – Anna was guileless and elegant, with a long, lean frame, while Avery was short, forceful and blunt – they found shared ground. Secretarial college was their way out. Anna did it as a condition of being allowed to go to art college – at least she'd have a proper qualification to fall back on when, the subtext suggested, she inevitably failed at art. Avery did the course to get a job, pay a mortgage, get the hell out. Anna was attracted to the way Avery completely lacked inhibition, because some days Anna felt nothing but inhibition.

'It's like an out-of-body experience. I'm watching myself being tidied away. It's what people will do when I'm dead,' says Avery.

'It's got sod-all to do with death, Ave,' says Anna, laughing. 'Go on.' She nods towards the shelves.

Avery stands on one of the wooden kitchen chairs, reaches up to the shelf, starts throwing things down directly into the bag.

'Can I at least send it to the charity shop?'

'Do what you want with it,' says Anna. 'Just get it out of here.'

'I hate this,' says Avery as she divides her things between bin, packing box and charity, but she keeps going until all that is left are two plates, a glass bowl and a couple of wine glasses for her to make lunch for them both.

Avery uses a fork and spoon to turn the salad leaves in the dressing. She is a terrible cook; she doesn't have the patience. So Anna always accepts whatever is placed in front of her. In this case, a bag of salad from the supermarket with shop-bought dressing squirted over it, a pre-cooked chicken, a loaf of bread. Avery puts it all on the table for Anna to help herself, but then hesitates, holding the plate with the chicken.

'Should I heat it?' she asks.

'It'll be fine,' Anna replies.

Anna sets out the plates, cutlery, a jug of water.

'I need some wine,' says Avery, pulling the cork out of a bottle of half-drunk Sauvignon Blanc from the fridge. She pours Anna a glass, which Anna drinks, more quickly than she usually would. They tear pieces from the chicken – the meat comes away in dry, stringy strips – and Avery keeps drinking, topping up Anna's glass, until a new bottle is opened, and the packing comes to a halt because Avery's too drunk and Anna's so lightheaded she can't get up from the armchair. So they give up, and spend the rest of the day lying on Avery's sofa, listening to her jazz collection, finishing off the wine. There's still time for packing.

A week later, David begins a sabbatical from work. They've packed up the house, which meant little more than switching off the boiler, emptying the fridge and freezer and debating about whether to take the cat with them. In the end, they decided the cat was too temperamental, too highly strung to cope with being taken away from her street, so Anna bought her a three-month supply of food, a furry new bed as a treat and asked the neighbour, Jane, to look after her.

She kisses the cat, closes the shutters in the sitting room, and they leave the life that Anna has been wedded to for the past thirty years, under the impression that the complication of leaving it is the reason they don't go anywhere for longer than a fortnight. In all those years, she's only once been away for more than that. When her mother was dying, she stayed away for a month.

Anna sits beside David in the car, feeling uneasy. She sends Avery a text message: *What if we never leave?*

You can do as you please, comes the reply, *leave whenever you want*.

Anna's stomach feels shot through with nerves. The road's signposts signal The North: to Anna it feels like a death sentence.

They arrive late at a bed and breakfast in Cumbria, resume their journey first thing. By mid-afternoon the next day, they're at the ferry in Scotland, only to find it won't run until the weather improves. They book a room above a pub – threadbare pink carpet, yellow curtains, a bed that sags in the middle. At breakfast the next morning, the landlady puts a steel teapot on their table, points to the window and the blue sky beyond. 'You'll be all right today. The boats will go,' she says.

'I didn't realise we couldn't rely on the boats,' says Anna, as they drive on to the ferry that will take them to the island. 'What if there's an emergency?'

'See it as part of the adventure,' replies David.

It's cold, so they stay in the car for the journey. When they disembark, they weave their way down small coastal roads that grow more narrow, more rough, more remote, until they arrive at the house. Anna stretches, takes in deep breaths of fresh, clean air. Her body opens and unwinds after all the hours of sitting. They ring the doorbell and Jerri appears, telling them it wasn't locked, they should have come straight in.

'We didn't like to barge in,' says Anna.

Jerri puts the kettle on. David leaves Anna with his mother while he goes back outside to unload the car. Jerri begins to chatter, asking about their journey: was there any traffic? Did they remember the way? When the tea's ready, Jerri takes them into the sitting room. More than three months since the accident, and Rachel's reading glasses still rest on top of a book. A stack of magazines is pushed up against the side of a chair. Peter's green gardening coat hangs by the window. An old mobile phone on the marble mantelpiece reminds Anna that hers is in her pocket. She checks it.

'No signal here, remember? You'll have to go up to the cairn at the top of the hill, close to the farm track if you want to use your mobile. But there's the landline.' Jerri nods towards the phone on the dresser.

Anna puts away her mobile. 'The girls?' she asks. 'How are they?'

'Asleep,' says Jerri. 'They didn't sleep much last night.'

Anna's eyes flicker through the sitting room window, scanning the view towards the woods, the sea running around the edges of the landscape.

'I prepared your room. The door at the top of the landing. The one with the three windows and the balcony. The nicest room, I think,' says Jerri.

Anna had hoped to stay in the room they'd used before, the one with the old brass bed and peacock wallpaper, but Jerri has decided otherwise, and Anna will do as she's told.

'I thought you'd be happiest in there. The view is lovely,' says Jerri. 'And it gets the best of the morning light. Once Michael left, I took the small room, next to the girls, because they were having so much difficulty overnight. But there's only a single bed in there, so it wouldn't do for you and David.'

Anna fetches her case from the hall, takes it upstairs, wondering if she should analyse the fact that Jerri has chosen for her son and his wife a bedroom with two single beds, when there are two other rooms, just as nice, with double beds. Should she let her mind wander down that avenue? Sex and the family? No! She'll unzip her case, put her things in the drawers and allow Jerri her triumph over David's body.

The room's central window is arched and grand, opening out on to a crumbling stone balcony with a view of the river. Inside, there's an enormous Regency wardrobe, inlaid with mother-of-pearl, along with an ornate marble fireplace, a marble-topped dressing table with a gilt mirror, and a bow-fronted chest of drawers into which she'll transfer her clothes. On the wall above the fireplace is a triptych of photographs. The first, a panoramic view of sea and cliffs. The next, an image of sky meeting sea, but when Anna looks more closely, she notices a tiny figure flying through the air. She realises that it's Rachel, who had belonged to a group of twenty athletes and campaigners who 'wild dived'. They reclaimed water, took over cliffs marked out of bounds, or corners of lakes, to prove a point about whom the world belonged to. The last time Anna and David had visited, Rachel had just secured some corporate sponsorship to pay for her group to travel to Australia. She'd prepared her pitch for weeks. She was worried she wouldn't get it, but it seemed so obvious to Anna. Rachel would have those men in suits eating out of her hand, which is, of course, what happened. When they opened a bottle of champagne to celebrate, Peter said: 'It's ironic that corporate money will be spreading the word about corporations invading our last remaining wild spaces. They'll make you throw

yourself off a cliff with their logo attached to your forehead.'
He was snide, belittling. Anna hadn't seen this side of Peter
before. David intervened to calm things down between
them. But still, Rachel was annoyed. She took herself away
for the rest of the evening, claiming she had a headache.

In the third photograph, Rachel is unfurling herself over
a Tanzanian lake. Anna remembers Peter trying to persuade
her not to do it. He was worried about crocodiles, but
Rachel wouldn't hear of it. She argued back: they'd done
their research. She knew she'd be fine. She craved risk. She
wanted to defy the world, to go to places humans weren't
welcome, doing things that most people couldn't physically
do.

Opening her suitcase, Anna realises she's forgotten so
many things. No woolly hat, no gloves, no scarves, nothing
warm to wear in bed. Only one thick sweater. What was
she thinking? Even from the other side of the room, she can
feel the icy draught from the window. Anna finds herself in
Rachel's bedroom, picking her way through the drawers in
search of something warm to borrow. She finds a pair of
thick, grey socks, a scarf, then spots an Aran sweater,
folded up and pushed to the back with the labels still on.
She removes them, slips the sweater over her head.

In the sitting room, Jerri is pouring out tea for David.
The string of blue beads at Jerri's neck, the burgundy
cardigan, cream blouse and navy-blue tapered trousers
make her seem so warm and predictable. If Jerri stayed,
Anna wouldn't have to do all this work. She could play the

role of little girl, let herself be mothered. Once the tea is poured, Jerri brings out several sheets of paper. 'The handover,' she says.

First one: the battle to keep the house warm. She's written notes on where to find the logs, what to do when they run out, the location of the electric radiators, the boiler, how to switch everything on and off. Another list explains the location of the fuse box, water mains, nearest shop for milk and bread.

'Come and sit down, David,' says Jerri. 'These are important things to know.'

But David isn't listening.

'You have to know how to run the place. It'll fall apart around your ears if you don't pay attention and work at it,' says Jerri.

'I'm listening,' says Anna.

Jerri hands Anna the document. Her neat, straight handwriting lists the bullet points. Things the girls will eat; things to keep everyone occupied; things to do when the weather is bad; how to work the thermostat.

David puts his empty cup on the coffee table. 'Are you staying tonight?' he asks.

'I have to get back. For Michael,' says Jerri.

'But we've only just got here. You can't leave.'

'Yes,' says Anna. 'Don't rush off.'

But Jerri has already spent three months at the house. It's too much. Michael left a week ago, she's been alone up here for six nights. She needs to get home. Michael said she shouldn't drive in the dark on these unlit roads. The ferries are running today. They might not be tomorrow. If she gets the afternoon ferry, she should at least get to the motorway before night falls. David protests, but Jerri stands firm: she's not going to be pushed around by her own son. The list of reasons continues. 'I promised him I'd be home tomorrow, and I can't do the whole drive in one go,' she says. 'But I'll come and stay again. I'll bring your father. You'll be OK,' she says. 'You'll both be OK.'

She stands up, takes her suitcase, walks out the door and is gone.

'Should we wake them?' Anna asks.

'Let them sleep,' says David. He is crouching in the brick fireplace, trying to light a fire.

'Surely we should wake them? They won't sleep tonight,' says Anna, as she searches the fridge for something to make for supper. 'There's not much in here.'

She spots a head of broccoli, some Cheddar, a half-eaten tub of cream cheese, a punnet of tomatoes. In the cupboards are pasta, rice, couscous. She tries to think of something she can cook, but realises she doesn't want to eat any of it. She picks up her handbag. 'I'm going to the shop to fetch something.'

'There must be enough food in,' David replies, standing up from the fire.

'You've still got the car keys,' Anna says, holding out her hand.

'We don't need food. Not tonight. Not when it will be dark soon.'

'We do,' Anna says. 'The girls will need to eat too. There's no milk, either. No bread.'

'My mother wouldn't have left us with nothing. There'll be something,' David says.

'But David . . .'

Anna knows David has the car keys in his pocket. But David keeps saying that she ought to stay. Anna will never find the local shop. She'll get lost on the way back. The roads aren't lit. And anyway, he isn't that hungry. 'I'd be worried about you if you left now,' he says.

Anna can see the outline in his pocket. It's a shared car; he can't just *take* it. 'Can I have the keys?' she asks.

'Here, look!' he says, lifting the lid of a white dish resting on the counter. 'Fish pie. My mother left us a fish pie.'

Anna puts the pie in the oven while David pours the wine. She lays the table for four, but when the food is ready, the girls are still not awake, so they sit in the kitchen on unsteady wooden chairs and eat in silence.

Afterwards, they sit by the fire in the sitting room. Everywhere in this room there are signs of the bitter coldness to come. Piles of thick woollen blankets, huge baskets full of logs, heavy curtains, sausage-shaped stuffed toys at the base of the doors. David says tomorrow he'll bring in logs to stack by the fire. Anna wonders if she should have brought the cat. A doughnut of warm fur in her lap would be nice. She wraps herself in one of the blankets. David has a book open in his lap. He puts it aside, teases the fire with a long iron poker. Anna abandons her spot on the sofa, sits next to David on the hearth. She's hugging her knees to her chest, feeling the flames warm her up, when the sitting room door flies open and both girls appear in the room.

'Where's Granny?' says Isabella. She's a mixture of fury and vulnerability that catches Anna off guard. She'd been settling in for a quiet evening in front of the fire. She hadn't expected their new life together to happen like this, with such force.

'She's gone home,' says David. 'We're here to look after you now.'

The flesh of Isabella's cheeks collapses. 'She didn't say goodbye? Why didn't she wake us?'

'You did know we were coming today?' says Anna.

'Yes,' replies Sasha.

'But we didn't know Granny was going to be gone by the time we woke up,' wails Isabella.

'Yes, we did,' says Sasha.

'She told us she said goodbye before you both went for your nap. She said you'd had a bad night's sleep, and needed to take a nap, and she told you she'd be gone when you woke because she didn't want to drive in the dark,' says Anna.

Anna is confused by the speed at which Jerri left. Jerri had assured them both she'd prepared the girls for their change in circumstances, that they knew she was going but would be back. Rather than gently slipping into their lives,

Anna and David have been dropped like bombs into the middle of it all. They are all laid bare. The girls are confused and angry. Anna is finding it hard to know what to say to make things better.

But then Sasha, who is quieter and more tentative than Isabella, goes towards Anna. She kisses her. It feels like a truce, but Isabella is still distant and aloof, determined not to back down on her fury. Anna doesn't want to begin like this. She doesn't want to quarrel, or to fail so she attempts to smooth things over.

'I'm sorry you're upset,' she says. She tries to hug Isabella, but feels the resistance in her body and immediately lets her go. Isabella's eyes flicker from David to Anna, then back again: a fragile, accusing look, full of mistrust.

'Are you hungry? Jerri has left you both something to eat.'

Feeding. This she can do. The girls follow Anna into the kitchen, where she removes the lid from the dish of fish pie. Sasha looks inside, screws up her face. Isabella doesn't even look.

'We're not very hungry,' says Sasha.

'You must try and eat something,' says Anna. 'You'll feel better if you eat.'

'But not fish,' says Isabella. 'I can't stomach fish. The smell of it is making me feel queasy.'

Anna opens up the fridge, offers them whatever they want. They sit at the table, their feet propped on chairs, ask for yoghurt. Anna fetches them some spoons. Isabella chooses a banana from the bowl on the table. She peels it, munches through the fruit, then tosses the skin through the air. From where she is sitting, it lands on top of the bin.

'You look like you've done that before,' says Anna.

'I have a good aim,' replies Isabella.

'Perhaps it's a good thing for the rabbits and birds round here that your parents didn't like guns,' says Anna. 'Otherwise you'd have been out there . . .' Isabella gets up from the table to fetch a yoghurt. Anna's voice trails off. She has no idea why she said that. Isabella hands Sasha another pot of yoghurt.

'What makes you think my parents didn't like guns?' says Isabella.

'I just assumed . . .'

'We've got a cupboard full of them,' says Sasha. 'Isabella's an amazing shot. She used to shoot with Daddy all the time.'

Jerri is right. They do look too thin. Their eyes are sinking into their faces. They're pale, far too pale. Sasha gobbles up the last of her yoghurt, taking quick, tiny mouthfuls. At the bin, she rescues the banana skin from the lid, drops it inside along with her empty yoghurt pot, then returns to the table. She slips in beside Isabella, who is leaning back with her legs resting on the corner of the table. There's an insolence to the way she is sitting: her long neck arched back so that she looks at Anna through half-closed eyes, her legs lolling across the corner of the dining table. If it had been one of her own sons, Anna would have pushed his legs down, told him off, but she senses Isabella's vulnerability and says nothing.

Before these girls were born, Rachel had so many miscarriages, so much heartache, so many tears, that when Isabella was finally born, and then Rachel fell pregnant again only two months later, she always said she felt something bigger than herself at play: a divine reward for her suffering. Anna thought it a load of nonsense – Rachel was into this pseudo-spirituality, which she put down to her Californian upbringing – but now she is beginning to wonder if Rachel was right. Somehow, the girls knew of the trouble that lay ahead, knew they'd need to be a pair.

Anna tries again with Isabella. 'I'm here to look after you. It's what I promised your parents, and it's what I'm going to do.'

Isabella says nothing. They sit in silence, awkwardly avoiding the other's gaze, until David arrives to rescue the situation: 'How about a movie?' he says, holding his laptop and a cardboard box containing discs. 'I've found films in a cupboard upstairs. We can play them on my computer.'

The girls hesitate. They're being pushed into forbidden territory. Rachel had strict rules about television and the internet.

'As a treat,' says David.

'We weren't allowed to watch this stuff all the time,' says Sasha.

'You'll enjoy it,' he replies.

The girls follow David into the sitting room. The three

of them take up their positions on the sofa. David opens the box. The girls look inside, reluctantly at first, then Sasha spots something. Her hands dive into the box. She pulls out an American teen film, holds it up to show Isabella. Isabella nods. David puts the disc into the computer, sets it up on the coffee table. The girls curl into their seats, lean against one another while David fusses. He cleans the screen with his sleeve, worries whether both of them can see, changes the angle of the lamp to stop the reflection. Will they let him know if they don't like the film? He can put something else on. Should he put another log on the fire? Should he fetch a blanket? No longer an uncle, but a father again, twitching and worrying in a way he hadn't done with his own sons, because that was Anna's role; fussing was what she did.

While David sets up the film, Anna goes around locking the doors, ensuring the windows are closed. A habit from London, perhaps. Who's going to climb in here? And what would they take, anyway? Both girls are cuddled into David's chest. Isabella is playing with his fingers, rubbing each one between her own, examining them individually. 'Your hands are just like Daddy's,' she says. Sasha rests her head in David's lap, his arm loosely around her waist. The girls have colonised him, like two strands of ivy growing over him, claiming him as their own. No room for Anna, so she takes an armchair by the fire. As the film wears on, she feels sympathy with Rachel. Who would want their daughters watching this rubbish? She bristles at its cynicism,

at the stuff it's teaching these girls about life and relationships – everything is so transactional these days, their
bodies no more than commodities they can use to barter –
but she sits it out. Sasha and Isabella seem surprised and
delighted when the two protagonists finally get over the
obstacle thwarting their love, and kiss. Anna is longing for
sleep, longing for the film to be over. When finally it ends,
she tells the girls they should go to bed. Isabella sleepily
disentangles herself from David, yawns.

'I won't sleep,' she replies. 'The nights are too empty.'

But Sasha is already asleep, her head still in David's lap.
He cradles her neck with one arm, slides the other beneath
her legs, carries her up the stairs with Anna following.
Sasha murmurs as he lays her in bed. He pulls the covers
up around her, tucks her in. Isabella clambers in next to
her sister.

'You know where we are,' says Anna, sitting on the edge
of the bed. 'If you're scared, just shout and we'll come. And
perhaps tomorrow you can show me your island?'

'I don't want to go to sleep,' says Isabella.

'You'll feel better if you do.' Anna switches the light off.

In their own bedroom, David swears as he fiddles with
the notch on the radiator, trying to get it to budge in the
hope of a little heat. Anna is undressing when, without
warning, Sasha appears in their room.

'Isabella's been sick. Really sick. Everywhere.'

In her bedroom, Isabella is on the floor, holding her
stomach. Her teeth chatter, a long line of saliva dangles

from her mouth. She's groaning, rocking back and forth. Sasha crouches beside her, rubbing her back, trying to talk to her, but Isabella won't speak. Is she in pain? She nods. David fetches her a glass of water, some paracetamol, while Anna takes her to the bathroom to wash.

She helps Isabella to undress, but then hesitates. Should she stay? Or allow her privacy? Is she a girl or a young woman? Isabella seems to notice Anna's indecision, because she asks her to stay. 'Please,' she says. 'I don't want to be on my own.'

Anna squeezes warm water from the sponge down Isabella's back. Her stick arms hug her stick legs. She's shivering. Anna keeps working the warm water along her body. When she's clean, Anna fetches a bath towel, helps her out of the bath, wraps her up. In the bedroom, Isabella puts on fresh nightclothes. Anna smooths down the clean sheets. She turns the corner of the covers back. Isabella gets into the bed. Anna covers her up, tucks her in, smooths her hair one more time, tells her she'll be back in five minutes. Downstairs, she makes a pot of mint tea, which she takes up for Isabella.

'This will help your stomach,' she says. 'And sleep. You must get some sleep.' She turns the bedroom light off, closes the door, reminding the girls again that she is not far away if they need anything.

'Isabella's worrying me,' says Anna to David once they are alone in their room again.

'It'll pass,' replies David.

'This isn't a stomach bug,' says Anna.

'Let's wait and see.'

'She needs help.'

'I'll stay in their room overnight,' says David, getting out of bed.

They drag a single mattress on to the floor of the girls' room, make up the bed.

'I'm going to be here all night, girls,' David says.

They don't reply. They're already asleep, with Sasha's arm resting over her sister's belly. Their soft faces nestle into the pillow, mouths rounded as they breathe, not in synchrony but mis-stepping. The crinkle of contempt that usually curls around Isabella's eyes and forehead is smoothed away.

'I just want them to be OK,' David says.

When Anna awakes, Rachel is opposite her, somersaulting through hot, tropical air. It's not a good start to the day. Anna's joints ache, her nose feels as if it has been dipped in ice. She slept fitfully, woken constantly by the cold.

Downstairs, the day is unfolding. A mist is giving way to a soft pink light pouring over the landscape. A line of bare trees is picked out by that light, making them look like solid amber. The sun dapples the kitchen. The room feels cheerful and inviting. Anna takes a mug of tea outside. Droplets of moisture cling to the grass and shrubs. Her shoes gather damp grass as she walks. Silence. Absolute silence. It's a vast, unfilled space. A place where you might slip away from ordinary life. In London, there is no time for anything, but up here, there's nothing but time. Anna carries on through the garden. She has never envied Rachel this life. So much work, just for a place to live. Every time they came to stay, Rachel would be hard at it, tending. Usually by now, the garden would be prepared for the harsh winter. Plants cut right back to the ground, ferns wrapped in their protective covers, the more vulnerable plants taken into the greenhouse in their pots. Anna was amazed at how productive Rachel was – surprised, in fact, that she had it in her. As she walks around the garden, she keeps spotting things that need doing. A shrub lies on its side – dug up by an animal? She kicks it away into the undergrowth, then pulls a set of rusting croquet hoops out of the lawn, untangles a blue plastic bag caught in the low branches of a tree.

Anna stops at the pond. Jutting out on to the kidney-shaped pool of water is a small wooden pontoon that Rachel used to lie on in summer. All around the water's edge, she planted a dense garden – *Fatsia japonica*, *Gunnera*, ferns, hostas – so that the water feels as if it's nestling within a jungle. At the far corner is the upturned body of a dead carp. Its white fleshy belly slaps against the bank.

Rachel used to disappear to this pond and lie on a mattress, smoking and reading all day, hidden away among the glossy leaves of the undergrowth. One time, Anna and David went with her – David even swam – bobbing along beside Rachel as she undulated through the water like a piece of silk being pulled. David managed two lengths, then hauled himself out, his legs covered in algae, green cobwebs that he picked off in threads. Sasha was young at the time, two or maybe three years old, certainly no more. She was always clambering on her mother, pawing at her, this unquenchable desire to touch her, and Rachel let her. Both girls had the run of her body – she never batted them away, never grew irritated, as if it was her fate to be admired. What was the point in being this beautiful if you denied yourself to others? Anna remembers a time when Sasha pulled her mother's bikini right down, tugged it away with her tiny, clumsy hands. A glittering mauve bikini with a tiny thread that went round her neck to keep it in place. Sasha pushed her mother's nipple, then giggled. Rachel barely noticed, she carried on reading her book, but David was transfixed by the scene. He stared at his brother's wife's breast, this child clambering up her body. Anna had felt hurt: he wasn't normally the type to leer at women. 'What do you think of Rachel?' she'd asked him later when they were alone.

'She's nice,' he'd said. 'Very young, but she suits Peter. He seems happy.'

Anna used to feel jealous of Rachel because she radiated a kind of promise, particularly in summer, when she looked even more golden than usual. It was hard not to want to reach out and test the softness of her skin. Those eyes, the grace in her movements. She seemed to have an awareness of herself as a lusciously feminine, self-consciously rebellious, piece of theatre. Anna often felt lacking when she was around Rachel. When they swam in the sea, Rachel would swim out further than anyone else. When they went out walking, she wouldn't go around the rocks that peppered the hill as everyone else would; she'd tackle them, clambering up them, her strong, muscular legs propelling her to the top and over. She had a defiance towards the world. These obstacles weren't simple accidents of creation, but a challenge – as if she took the whole world personally. She must prove to it she was stronger, better, brighter.

Anna drains her tea, goes back inside. Her first job will be to buy food. In the bedroom, she finds David's trousers hanging over a chair, slips her hand into the pocket, navigates her way around a dirty handkerchief, some loose change, finds the car keys.

She takes the ferry. Halfway out to sea, her phone comes alive. A message from Avery asking for news. She replies: *Arrived. It's quiet. Lots of sea. Lots of seagulls. Not much else. How's the new house?*

A reply comes straight back: *I fucking hate it. Wish I'd never moved. Nowhere to get a decent coffee. Nosy neighbours.*

Another text message comes in, this time from Andrew, wanting to know how everyone is. Anna replies *We're all fine*, but something about the message makes her worry about him – he's not usually this concerned with everyone – so she calls him, leaves a message to tell him she's worried, he can call the landline if he wants to talk.

At the supermarket, it's quiet. Anna barely thinks as she travels through the shop, picking things off the shelves. By the time she reaches the checkout, her trolley is overflowing with stuff she can't remember putting in. Double-chocolate cookies? Her unconscious's idea of what teenage girls like. She hands over her credit card, stacks the bags into the back of her car, begins her drive back.

At the port, she notices a greasy spoon café. Through its tiny, steamed-up windows, she sees the fishermen and decides to go inside. They stare at her as she finds a seat, orders a mug of tea, speaking quietly as if that will mask her English accent. But no one engages with her. The men carry on eating their breakfasts, yellow oilskin coats trailing on the floor from the backs of their chairs. Anna wonders if she's broken an unwritten rule that women shouldn't come into this place, but then the door opens and a loud woman in a pink anorak enters. She fills the space with the strength of her movements, the intensity of her bellowing voice, as she makes her way up to the till to order. The air is fatty, full of steam, but it's warm, and outside this place everywhere is cold and hard. Beyond the built-up wall of the docks, jagged black rocks line the sea, the trawlers knock side to side in the swell. The men are hard, the weather's hard, the sea is black and cold.

Driving home, Anna is lost in thought – will her cat be OK? will Jane always remember to feed her? – and, too late, she realises she's almost missed the turning into the driveway. She brakes suddenly, swinging sharply to the right. A bag on the backseat falls forwards, spilling its contents. She turns to push the bag upright, still driving, but the sound of something hitting the car is so loud Anna shrieks. She rams her foot on to the brake pedal. The car stops with a force that plunges the remaining shopping bags on to the floor.

Anna opens the door. Her heart hammers. Coming from beneath the car is a frantic, desperate sound. Wings flapping. Anna freezes, stuck to her seat. The sound begins to grow softer, fading gradually. There is a whimpering; a soft, pained moan. Anna doesn't move. Finally the sounds dwindle to nothing. The wings come to a rest against the tarmac. Anna's hands shake as she steps out of the car. Her breathing is quick and shallow. Up from London. Clueless. Already, the countryside has turned her into a murderer. She has no idea what you are meant to do with a dead pheasant. She peeks underneath the car. It's lying limp against the tarmac. She's never seen one so close. Deep iridescent purple-blue around its neck that turns gradually more green – the colours of a peacock – then a bright white feathered collar. Along its body, delicate colours are hidden within the auburn and brown. Soft green, pink, a gentle turquoise. How could she have done this to something so beautiful? She looks around to check that no one has seen her, puts her foot against it, using short kicks to bring it into the open. Bloodied beak gaping, the body floppy and soft. She daren't touch it, but she can't leave it there, either.

She uses a plastic shopping bag, dips her hand inside to grab the neck of the bird, drags it into the woodland. She kicks away the leaves from underneath a beech tree, pushes the dead bird into the clearing, covering its body with leaves, all the time feeling a sharp pang of regret. Hopefully a fox will get it and her inadequacy will be concealed.

Back at the house, the girls are watching another film with David. Anna puts the shopping away, goes up to their room to tidy it, picking up the clothes scattered on the floor: knickers, little lace bras in neon yellow and pink, jeans and tiny T-shirts. She gathers them up, takes it all downstairs to wash.

And this is how she spends her first day up at the house. Hidden away like a servant in the windowless utility room, doing the laundry. The walls are made of crumbling brick, roughly whitewashed. The room is damp, muggy. The washing machine churns and spins. Maybe she should sit on it, jiggle herself about like an old-fashioned housewife. The machine builds up in speed, making its crescendo towards its final break-neck spin. Anna watches it vibrate. When the clothes are all washed and dried, she folds them and puts them away. She's Rachel's hired help. Too old to be a cute and forgivable servant girl, she'd be the house-keeper, the old matron. Thick-waisted, with fingers like fat, pink sausages from all the hard work

The path on the hill is no more than a vein of bare earth running through the heather. Anna walks with her eyes to the ground, searching out the rocks and holes so she doesn't trip. Ahead of her, the girls expertly leap across anything the hill puts in their way. They seem happy up here with the wind knocking against them. Below, the sea is a circle of ink-blue, widening out into open sea. The trees edging the coast cushion the harsh, rocky edge of the water, making it seem soft, inviting. The higher up the hill they go, the smaller the roads criss-crossing beneath them seem. Sasha points to the tiny village on the shore – nothing more than a few small, brightly coloured boxes wedged in between sea and rock.

'Two hours there. Two hours back. We used to walk there all the time to buy sweets. Isabella would take money from Daddy's pocket,' says Sasha.

'Come on,' replies Anna. 'I'll buy you each a bag of sweets for old times' sake.'

They start to follow the path to the village, but then the rain starts. The girls yell to Anna to follow them to shelter beneath a patch of pine trees. In the glade, Anna sits with her back against the rough bark of the tree, picks up handfuls of brown fallen needles, lets them tumble between her fingers. As she watches the rain, she breathes in the fresh smell of pine and damp from her shelter. Over time, the rain moves across the sea in a column of blurred grey. They emerge from the trees, fumble their way back across the wet heather.

At the village, an old brass bell clangs as the door of the shop slams shut behind them. Jars of sweets are lined up on a shelf. Anna gives the girls each a pound and they seem excited, which confounds her. Aloof teenagers haughtily staring her down one day; the next, they're little girls excited about penny sweets. Isabella goes first: sherbet lemons, Black Jacks, pear drops. The shopkeeper shakes them out on to the scales, then decants them into a small white bag, which she hands to Isabella. Next, it's Sasha's turn: milk bottles, fudge, white mice.

'White mice?' says Isabella. 'I didn't see them.' She looks at Anna in the hope of more money, but Anna doesn't have enough. She wants to buy sandwiches – the girls can't just eat sweets for lunch – and she gave them her last two pound coins.

'We'll share,' says Sasha. She opens her bag of sweets, lets Isabella pick out some of the white mice.

'You haven't left me any,' Sasha complains.

'Yes, I have.'

Sasha inspects the bag: none left.

'Don't argue, girls,' says Anna.

Isabella holds out her palm to Sasha, who plucks two mice from it, drops them back into her bag. Outside, they sit on the low wall in front of the sea, their feet dangling against the black rock sloping towards the sea. The two girls sit beside Anna, gobbling up their sandwiches, squabbling over the sweets. She feels nostalgic: she's a mother again. It's not so bad.

The girls want to row home, to show Anna the view of the cliffs from the sea. They go together to the house of their mother's friend Irene, to ask if they can borrow her rowing boat. Ten minutes later, they return with the key to the padlock.

'She says we can use it on the condition we re-paint it,' says Sasha.

The three of them clamber down the rocks, pick their way along the shore towards the jetty, where they find the small wooden boat tied up. Isabella unlocks the padlock, pulls the chain through the steel ring, holds on to it while Anna and Sasha step into the boat, jumping in after them. Two benches: one in the middle where the girls sit; one at the end that Anna takes. As Isabella arranges the oars in the rowlocks, she drops one of them, trapping the side of her hand between sharp metal and heavy oar. She yelps, bites her lip to stop herself from crying. Eventually she lets Anna examine her hand. Blood trickles down Isabella's palm as Anna looks at it. 'It's a deep wound,' says Anna, pulling a tissue from her bag. She wraps it around Isabella's hand, pressing hard to stop the bleeding, while Isabella sits in silence, determined not to cry.

Injured, Isabella lets Anna row while Sasha holds the tiller. She steers them past the end of the jetty, into the bay and out to sea. All the time, Isabella nurses her wound, holding it firmly to stop the bleeding. The sea laps at the boat, knocking them gently from side to side. Grey clouds swell in the distance.

'We'll be home by the time the rain starts,' says Isabella.

'You look worried,' says Sasha to Anna.

'This weather,' says Anna. 'It's always there in the background, like a threat.'

'You'll get used to it,' she replies. 'Mummy hated it at first. She wanted to go home, but in the end, she loved the wildness of the weather more than anything.'

They edge along the sandy curve of the beach until the bay ends, then begin the more treacherous journey around the base of a cliff, where the sea is choppier. The girls stare idly out to sea; none of this worries them. At the cliffs, the water explodes against the rocks, sending up white spray. Anna feels nervous, tries not to show it. When, finally, they round the cliffs and begin inching back towards the beach, she feels relief.

'Can I see your hand?' asks Sasha.

Isabella carefully unwinds the tissue. Most of the side of her hand is covered in dried blood.

'Does it still hurt?' Sasha asks.

Isabella nods. 'It needs cleaning,' she says. She leans over the boat, dips her hand into the sea. She winces as the salt hits, then runs the forefinger of her other hand delicately over the wound, dissolving the blood away. Cleaned, the wound is shiny and pink. A neat slit that runs through the flesh between her thumb and forefinger. Anna gives her another tissue. Very carefully, Isabella dabs the wound dry, then wraps her hand up again as if this wound were a precious object she's preserving.

They make it back in half the time it took to walk. At the jetty, they tie up the boat, jump on to the rocks, clamber ashore. Inside the house, they light a fire in the library. Isabella lies on her belly on the marble hearth, feet kicking in the air, turning the pages of a photograph album. Next to her, Sasha copies out a poem from an old volume she's pulled down from the shelf. She swirls the ends of the letters 'y' and 'g' into long, decorative coils.

'It's Wordsworth. Mummy's favourite from *The Prelude*. Shall I read it out?'

Anna nods. Sasha stands, her expression serious. She draws a deep breath and begins:

> *One summer evening (led by her) I found*
> *A little boat tied to a willow tree*
> *Within a rocky cove, its usual home.*
> *Straight I unloosed her chain, and stepping in*
> *Pushed from the shore. It was an act of stealth*
> *And troubled pleasure, nor without the voice*
> *Of mountain-echoes did my boat move on;*
> *Leaving behind her still, on either side,*
> *Small circles glittering idly in the moon,*
> *Until they melted all into one track*
> *Of sparkling light.*
> *But now, like one who rows,*
> *Proud of his skill, to reach a chosen point*
> *With an unswerving line, I fixed my view*
> *Upon the summit of a craggy ridge,*
> *The horizon's utmost boundary; far above*
> *Was nothing but the stars and the grey sky.*

Sasha lays down the piece of paper.

'Beautiful,' says Anna.

'Mummy loved poetry,' says Isabella.

The girls pull a small antique table over to the window. Sasha leans her poem up against a vase. Next to it, Isabella puts a photograph of both girls with their parents. From the drawer, they take out four candles, incense sticks. Together, they light the candles with a match, then use them to get the incense sticks burning. A blue coil of smoke wanders lazily among the display. When David comes in from chopping wood, he admires the girls' work.

'Brendan called,' he says to Anna. 'He's coming up. He's got time on his hands; says he'll come and help out. He's got a few things to organise first, but can be here by Thursday.'

'Brendan again,' sighs Anna.

'Don't be like that,' replies David. 'We need all the help we can get at the moment. We both ought to be grateful.'

'Who's Brendan?' Isabella asks.

'A very old university friend of ours. You might have seen him at the funeral? A lovely man who's coming to help us,' says David.

It's Thursday. Brendan calls to say he'll be with them in time for dinner. Anna prepares the red room: painted red walls, deep red Oriental rug, dark mahogany sleigh bed. As evening draws in, David lights fires, chills a bottle of white wine. When Brendan doesn't come, they try his phone. No answer, so David leaves a message, opens the wine; they'll continue their evening without him.

By eleven, Brendan is still not at the house. David is already in bed so Anna writes a note telling Brendan which room to sleep in, leaves the lights on in the hallway, goes to bed herself. Why is he always so unreliable? When she's awoken by car headlights sweeping around the walls of her bedroom, it's six in the morning. She goes downstairs, shines a torch for him to find his way inside where she makes tea. Inside, Brendan complains about his journey, blames his lateness on the timetables for the boats. They go when they want, regardless of the times it states they're meant to go. Brendan messily eats a roll spread with jam, while confiding in Anna that he's in trouble at work again. He'd used the word 'savage' in a lecture without context-ualising it; a slip of the tongue, it was obvious what he meant, but a student had complained. The faculty wouldn't tell him who the complainant was, but it doesn't matter; he knows exactly which spotty-skinned little shit-stirrer it was. The faculty head had accepted Brendan had made a mistake. She'd rolled her eyes about this skittish, over-sensitive student, but it was her duty to give Brendan a mild telling-off. Something about the whole thing had irritated Brendan profoundly, he told Anna. He'd lost his temper, started shouting. The department head had listened patiently, until, finally, she'd had enough. She'd shut him up by ordering him to take a few months of research leave to get himself back together. She'd said he sounded stressed.

'You've been fired?' Anna asks.

'Suspended,' says Brendan. 'I'm too old to be getting told off. I'm thinking of retiring. There must be more to life than teaching "Introduction to Anthropology" to first year students. Times are different. No one is interested in ideas any more. I'm worried that lethargy is taking over. Is this old age? Is this how it starts? I miss my younger self,' he says.

Here he is: failed again, thinks Anna.

On their way up to his bedroom, they pass through the small anteroom with its dark walls and green carpet, Brendan notices a chunk of plaster has fallen from the ceiling. Slim batons of old, grey wood are exposed, as if a small bomb has gone off above them.

'I can fix that,' he says.

Brendan pokes his head around the door of the girls' room. There they are, asleep, all mixed up together: limbs, hair, sheets, everything intertwined into one lump. On a mattress on the floor lies David, wrapped in a blanket, blending into the mess of the room as if it's the aftermath of a teenage party.

'We should wake him,' says Brendan.

'Let him sleep,' replies Anna. 'He needs the rest. He was awake a lot overnight.'

Finally, Anna takes Brendan to the red room. He steps in, but immediately recoils. It's a huge room. Too grand. Far too big. He doesn't need all that space. He'll never sleep. He'll get agoraphobic. He's not used to rooms on this scale. He wants something smaller. Anna takes him to the single room where Jerri slept. One wooden bed, a tiny window, old sheets decorated with a faded pattern of spring flowers. The yellow carpet is worn through, but Brendan is happy. 'It's just to sleep,' he says, placing his suitcase in the corner.

Anna leaves him so he can shower, but minutes later he's in the kitchen with just a towel around his waist. There is no hot water.

'You'll have to wait,' she says. 'It's timed.'

An hour later, after they've both showered, Brendan suggests a walk.

Brendan sets the pace, but Anna chooses the route. They head inland, down a path that tracks through the woods of silver birch and Scots pine, along the side of the hill. They pick their way around the rocks, heading back towards the shoreline in a loop. An old bridge takes them over an inlet, then back. They move at a pace, brushing against thick undergrowth that leaves trails of damp against their clothes. At the side of the footpath, Brendan points out the carcass of a rabbit, then a few metres along, a small bird, perhaps a partridge or a wood pigeon.

'I killed a pheasant yesterday,' says Anna.

'With your bare hands?' Brendan asks.

'I ran it over.'

Brendan shrugs.

'I feel terrible about it,' says Anna.

Again Brendan shrugs, keeps his eyes on the path,

spotting bleached bones. Anna hates seeing these carcasses, stripped of their flesh. Fragile bones rotting among the damp grass. Life up here moves on, leaving no trace. In the city, things matter. Things are recorded, jotted down, remembered. Everything is seen by someone within a city, there is always a witness, whereas in the countryside, things wither away, leak out of existence.

They hit upon a series of rocks that are too high to climb. They have missed a turning, so must go back on themselves. Brendan chatters. He's still angry at the boy who got him suspended: says he's got no imagination, no subtlety of thought, the only thing he understands is rules. Anna is used to Brendan's rants. No point telling him that the boy is young, still trying to make sense of the world, of where he fits into it. She knows she must stay quiet: Brendan's mood will pass. When they reach the pine woods again, they fall into silence. No path, so they pick their way around the trees, meeting and parting, looping through the wood. Their feet sink into the soft earth. Light dapples the ground beneath the bare, young trees. Their slim trunks, the smell of damp earth, the patches of blue sky visible through the canopy of the trees. Brendan looks upwards, taking in long, deep breaths. He seems relieved to be away from London, to breathe fresh air, to have space. When they reach the shore, the water is clear and shallow; the seabed is covered in pebbles. A group of tiny fish beat their way through the water.

'We swam here last summer,' Anna says. 'The four of us

swam together. It was the last day I spent with Rachel and Peter.'

Brendan puts his arm around Anna's shoulders, pulls her in towards him. 'It will all be OK,' he says.

'Will it?'

'Of course it will.'

'I worry about the girls.'

'They'll be OK.'

'Isabella is sick almost every night.'

'In time, it'll stop.'

'They need something to do. Have a routine, a focus.'

'Oh God, no,' says Brendan. 'They need a language. They're lost in a fog. They need help to find the right words to get out of it.'

Anna doesn't counter-argue. It's hardly even a disagreement, little more than an exchange of perspectives, yet Anna feels uneasy. Brendan is going to cause trouble. She wriggles free of his arm, and they walk back to the house in silence.

In the kitchen, Brendan fetches a brown paper bag full of mangos he bought on his way up, produces a pen knife from his pocket and peels a mango. The unpeeled fruit is slippery in his hand. He struggles to sink his teeth into it. Juice flows down his chin. He slurps it up with his tongue. He chomps another huge chunk of the mango, more juice that he sucks up. He wipes his mouth on his sleeve, repeating this biting and sucking, licking of the juice, working his way around the soft, slippery flesh of the fruit. Anna feels

81

sick. He's almost slobbering. He's such a pig; he's like an animal. The juice is dribbling down his chin, on to his shirt and, ultimately, on to the table. She fetches him a napkin, which she thrusts angrily in his direction.

'Brendan, you're being disgusting,' she says. 'Use a knife and fork. You're making me feel sick.'

He runs his tongue along his chin to catch the drops of juice. 'Sorry,' he says.

More tentatively, he nibbles at the remaining flesh, sucking and pulling until all that is left is the diamond-shaped white bone at the centre of the mango, which he puts into his mouth for one final suck. Anna is so repulsed, she has to look away.

'It's OK. I've finished,' says Brendan, taking the mango stone from his mouth, casting it on to the table in front of him. He pushes back his chair, wipes his mouth on his sleeve, lights up a cigarette. He's still smoking it when Sasha and Isabella come down.

'Girls, do you remember Brendan?' says Anna.

Isabella's gaze drifts over towards him. 'Hi,' she says, loftily.

'Hi,' says Sasha, turning to the fridge to search for orange juice.

'Hello girls,' says Brendan. 'Lovely to see you.'

The girls go about their business in silence. For a moment, it's awkward, until David comes down and the atmosphere changes. The two men hug. David pours Brendan some coffee, tells him how happy he is to see him.

He wants to show Brendan the garden. There's work to be done. The pond needs looking at. The plants need cutting back, preparing for winter. There are things in the house that need fixing.

At the pond, Brendan stands on one side, Anna on the other. There is still some of the lushness of summer left. The huge *Gunnera* plant fans out over the water. Beneath it, ferns, hostas, variegated ivy. Anna holds a long stick while Brendan guides her towards the upturned bodies of three dead carp – left a bit, right a bit – until she manages to tease the stick into the mouth of one of the fish, lodging the stick within its gill to get a firm grip. Watched by the girls and David, Anna pushes the dead carp towards the pontoon, navigating it through the greenery, managing to avoid it getting tangled. At the pontoon, Brendan is lying on his front, a bin bag open, waiting for it. Anna keeps working it towards him. The fish rolls and turns in the water. Its white stomach flips, revealing shiny orange and black scales, then flips back, white underbelly again. Anna picks her way along the dried mud of the bank. When she reaches Brendan, she flicks the fish into the bin bag. Like this, they work, until all four dead fish have been removed.

'Are we getting more?' Sasha asks.

But Brendan tells her it's not possible. The fish will just keep dying. The pond is overgrown, too much greenery suffocates them. They'll never survive it.

'But Mummy loved this pond.'

'We can't just let it waste away,' says Isabella.

'There's only one option,' says Brendan, pulling off his boots, rolling his socks away, unbuttoning his trousers.

'What are you doing?' shrieks Sasha.

'Brendan,' berates Anna.

But he ignores her, drops his trousers to the floor. With his sweater still on, he dips his toe into the cold, brown water, then yelps, pulls it out again. The girls laugh as he puts his hands on his head, glances in their direction, then jumps in. He sucks in his breath. As he lands, water splashes up, soaking his sweater. Standing waist deep, he pulls it over his head, throws it on to the bank, and stands in the water, hands back on his head. He begins to jump on the spot, panting, playing to the crowd. The girls laugh.

'I'll make sure you can have your fish, girls,' he says.

He wades across the pond towards the thickest area of greenery. Here, he plunges his arm underneath the water, wrestles with something. A moment later, his hand emerges with the dripping roots of a plant gripped in his fist. He throws it on to the bank, goes back under for more. One by one, he rips up the plants, throwing them on to a heap. When he's done, he wades back across the pond, gathering up stems that have floated free, pulling them behind him as he returns to the other side.

'That's it,' he says, standing at the pontoon. 'Give me your hand, Isabella.'

'No!' she replies.

He grabs her hand anyway. She struggles away from

him, still laughing, light-hearted, until Brendan grows impatient: 'I'm not going to hurt you. Just give me both hands.'

She gives in to him. With each hand firmly in his, he asks her to slip her feet out of her shoes, step on to his shoulders.

'You can say no,' says David, 'if you don't want to do it.'

But Isabella does want to. She puts one foot, then the other, onto Brendan's shoulders. Slowly, he turns and begins to walk across the pond with Isabella, a circus acrobat, balancing on his shoulders. Concentrating hard, he wades back through the water to the other side of the pond. Once he reaches the edge, he very slowly turns and walks back, letting Isabella jump on to the pontoon.

'Sasha?' Brendan says.

Gripping his hands, Sasha steps on to Brendan's shoulders. Again, he wades slowly through the water, but halfway across, Sasha panics. She doesn't like it, she might fall in, she wants him to take her back.

'You're fine,' he says, ignoring her, continuing to walk.

'No, Brendan,' says David, firmly. 'She doesn't like it. Bring her back.'

Brendan hesitates. 'Come on, Sasha,' he says gently. 'Just try it.'

'She doesn't want to do it,' says David.

'Once you do it, you'll like it,' says Brendan.

'Don't be a wimp,' shouts Isabella.

'No,' says Sasha. 'I don't like it and I want to get off.'

Very slowly, Brendan turns to take Sasha back to the pontoon. She steps off his shoulder, sits on the ground, angrily putting her shoes back on.

'I'll have another go,' says Isabella.

Isabella and Brendan cross the pond. This time, she pushes one leg out to the side, showing off. On her return, she takes her hands away from his, balances with her arms held out wide. Brendan ploughs up and down the water with Isabella until his teeth are chattering. His lips are turning blue. Finally, Isabella steps down from his shoulders. He hauls himself up on to the pontoon, grabs his clothes, runs inside for a hot shower.

It's five o'clock. Night is already with them: opaque and uncompromising, a thick black cloth thrown over the landscape, leaving only the sound of the waves and the wind. Anna draws the curtains. The fire David is trying to light begins to dwindle, then smokes and dies for the third time. He starts again, positioning twists of newspaper in the centre of the hearth. Painfully, carefully, piece by piece, he rests small sticks of kindling around it. Even more delicately, he rests a single larger log on top of this pyramid and strikes a match. Eventually, the fire takes on a life of its own. The kitchen feels warm. Brendan hands David a cold beer. Anna shouts upstairs to the girls that the food is ready. They come down, slip into their chairs. Anna passes around a bowl of buttered potatoes.

'I like your bracelets,' says Isabella, pointing to Brendan's thick forearms, which are covered in twenty, maybe more, braided bracelets, bright colours plaited together.

'These are from markets all over the world,' he says, holding his arm up so the girls can get a better look. They pick through them. Then he shows them a tarnished silver ring on his little finger. 'This, I got in Bali.' He spins the gold bands on his left thumb. The girls try to read the tiny etchings engraved into each band. 'These are from India. From a gold market in Delhi.'

He pulls off the gold rings, hands them to the girls, who take turns to examine the tiny Hindi letters. Next, he pushes up a sleeve, shows them a small tattoo of a bird on his forearm. 'This was done in Afghanistan. When you could still travel up there. I was only eighteen.'

'It's nice,' says Isabella. 'I want to get a tattoo one day.'

Brendan asks her what tattoo she'd like.

'A bird,' she says.

While the girls work out what kind of bird – an eagle? Too big. A hummingbird? Too exotic, too clichéd. Everyone would have a hummingbird. They'd like a gannet, in-flight, with his huge, black-tipped wings spread out across their skin.

When they finish eating, the girls drift back up to their bedroom. Brendan smokes one cigarette after another, until David finally tells him that Rachel and Peter didn't like smoking within the house. Brendan stubs out the cigarette, promises not to light another one, pours himself more wine. David tinkers with the fire. When the evening is eventually over, they count the bottles of wine. A horrible number to have drunk between three people. Brendan says he needs a cigarette, but it's raining. 'You can't send me out there,' he says.

'If you blow the smoke up the chimney, you can have one cigarette,' says David.

He agrees, has a last smoke before they decide together that it's time for bed. Upstairs, Anna completes her evening ritual of scrubs, creams and serums, while David sits propped up on a pillow, reading an old copy of *National Geographic* magazine. Then David has an idea. He rearranges the furniture to push their two beds together. When Anna climbs in, David shuffles out from underneath his blanket, puts a foot into her bed, then jumps in alongside her, almost causing Anna to fall out, but he catches her in time, then lays her on her back. Once she is stretched out beneath him, he holds her glance for a moment, gauging her mood. He kisses her breasts, moves his mouth towards her navel, then continues downwards. As she comes, she turns her head sidewards, glimpsing the sky through the open shutters. Wrapped up together in a single bed, warm and relaxed, David pulls her in more closely towards him. The rain is intensifying, bringing howling wind. The attic rattles and creaks. A door slams. David falls asleep immediately, but Anna can't. His grey hair falls across his eyes. His breath rises and falls. She feels an overwhelming love for him, for his form, for all that they are together; but also this terrible, tugging sense of disappointment that she doesn't understand. There are moments when married life feels like being contained inside a cylinder of very tight Lycra. She can move around, she can push against it, resist it, but she always feels constrained. Sometimes she enjoys, and needs, the constraint, because it contains her – contains both of them. Their lives don't fall about messily, in the way that Avery's and Brendan's do. But at other times, she could scream.

The door creaks, a shaft of light, a voice whispering: 'David, David. We're scared. We can't sleep.'

Anna feels the bed lighten as David rolls out of it. She hears him leave the room, then moments later, he returns. He pulls the mattress off his single bed, wrestling it out of the room. Anna doesn't like it on her own, all the creaking and rattling of the house. She feels scared. She wishes she could go and slip in beside David on his mattress on the floor, but instead she looks out at the canvas of stars from her bed. They seem to twinkle and shift in the wind. Eventually, she's carried off by sleep.

Brendan brings the waders, rods and nets to the back door. The girls find umbrellas and raincoats while he searches out the bright orange fishing tent in a cupboard in the cloakroom. They load the equipment on to the back of a flat wooden trailer attached to Peter's old tractor. Brendan drives, while the rest of them find a place to sit within all the stuff. They hold on tight, the girls' legs bouncing back and forth as the tractor rumbles down to the sea.

At the water, Brendan and David put up the tent. Anna throws a plastic sheet over the ground, while David uses old wooden crates to make small seats. He sets up a camping stove, a pan, a kettle, mugs for coffee. Anna complains of the cold, so David fetches her a woollen blanket. Draped in it, she watches while Brendan shows the girls how to attach tiny raw prawns to the hooks. A light drizzle begins to fall. Fishing. Pure misery.

'Cheer up,' says David.

'There's a reason we evolved,' says Anna.

'I find it hard to believe in progress,' replies Brendan.

'Progress has given us so many things,' says Anna.

'Progress has atomised us, made us lonely and miserable.'

'Central heating. Antibiotics,' says Anna.

'Antibiotics were the necessary solution to a man-made problem, created by progress because people were packed in tightly in unsanitary conditions in cities.'

'You're just making it up,' replies Anna. 'You're just shaping the past to mean whatever you want it to mean.'

'There are plenty of tribes still living without antibiotics.'

'If progress wasn't so wonderful, we would all have headed back to the woods,' says Anna.

'If it wasn't for the ruling classes—'

'You've lived with tribes?' asks Isabella, cutting Brendan off.

'Yes, many times,' says Brendan.

'Wow,' she says.

'The Hadza, the Yanomami, the Masai . . .'

'I've never even heard of any of them,' says Sasha.

'What was it like?' asks Isabella.

'Beautiful,' says Brendan. 'Witnessing the different forms humanity can take, how adaptable we are. There is no single meaning. Everything is a construct. Our brains are very flexible.'

The girls listen.

'Come on! Let's go,' he says.

Waders on, Brendan steps into the sea until the water is up to his waist. He's solid as he stands. The swift flow of the tide doesn't throw him off course as he casts his rod out to sea. The girls pull up the hoods on their coats. Sasha is the first to step out, followed by Isabella. They weave their way slowly out to Brendan, picking their way across the rocky ground beneath them. They stand beside him, holding out their rods. The girls are like reeds growing out of the sea, swaying with the ebb and flow of the current. Isabella's hair is just long enough that the tips rest in the water, flowing horizontally. The girls look so thin, so fragile against this solid, indubitable landscape.

'Are they safe out there?' says Anna.

'It's not deep,' says David.

Under the tarpaulin, David has a fire going. The rain makes a pleasing sound as it falls against the plastic sheeting.

Brendan shouts. He's caught something. David steps out to gather the fish from Brendan. A sea trout.

'It's illegal,' Brendan says, 'to catch them without a licence.'

'But who's going to know?' asks David, slicing its belly open, tipping its guts on to the sand. Then he dips it into the sea to take away the remains of stringy blood. Next, Sasha catches one, goes back to the tent to clean it. Finally, Isabella also lands a fish, takes her catch to David to prepare.

'I don't want to eat them,' Sasha shouts.

'You have to!' says Brendan.

'I don't want to eat something I've caught myself.'

'It's had a good life.'

'Still no,' says Sasha.

'They expect to be eaten. It's their destiny.'

By the time the girls have had enough – they're cold, it's not fun any more – there are eight fish, gutted and lined up, waiting to be cooked.

'Are you married?' Isabella asks Brendan.

'No,' he replies.

'Why aren't you married?' says Sasha.

'It's not something I've done,' says Brendan.

'Have you ever been married?' asks Isabella.

'No.'

'Do you have a girlfriend?'

'Not at the moment, but in the past I've had plenty of girlfriends.'

'Plenty?' the girls say simultaneously. They giggle.

'You must feel lonely without a girlfriend,' says Sasha.

'Well, sometimes, yes. It would be nice to have someone. During the week, I'm quite busy at work, but at the weekends, yes. It would be nice to share these things with someone.'

The girls stay quiet.

'But I have plenty of friends. I'm always off doing something.'

'Doesn't everyone want to have someone to love?' says Isabella.

'For lots of humanity through the ages, love had absolutely nothing to do with anything. It was about mating,' replies Brendan.

'Brendan, stop it,' says David.

'Mating?' The girls collapse into giggles again.

'Some languages don't even have a word for love.'

'There's no such thing as love?'

'It's not seen as a central concept. Their lives aren't built around it.'

'What did you do in these tribes? Why do you go?'

Brendan puts more wood on the fire. 'I don't any more. I went because I found it fascinating. I'm interested in people, in what we do, how we act, why we do what we do. I'm interested in the more formalised way they organise their lives. Rites of passage, for example. Defining the line between childhood and adulthood through ritual.'

'It's weird you're not married, though,' says Sasha.

Brendan laughs, pokes at the fire with a stick, changes the subject.

After lunch, they untie the rowing boat and drag it on to the beach, then turn it over so that it rests upside down on the sand: a wooden shell with its paint peeling away in flakes. Anna crackles a piece between her fingers, pulling it off the wood. It needs sanding. They'll have to buy special paint. Brendan suggests splitting into groups. He and David will go to the mainland to buy paint for the boat; Anna will take the girls to the neighbouring island where the garden centre is to buy new carp for the pond.

At the car, the girls can't decide who will sit in the front and who in the back, so eventually they both shuffle on to the backseat. Anna pulls out of the gate, heads to the harbour and on to the ferry. The heavy chains are hauled up. The engine spews out thick, black diesel fumes. They edge out of the harbour. On the other side, Isabella clambers into the front and uses the map on her phone to direct Anna right up to the door of the garden centre. A sign tells customers to push the bell if the door isn't open, so Anna rings. They wait. The girls paw at the tarmac with the toes of their trainers. A woman in a dark-blue husky jacket pokes her head around the door.

'Are you open?' asks Anna.

The woman lets them into the building. 'If you need help, my husband will come,' the woman says, then disappears again.

Anna and the girls wander past a display of rockeries, towards a large section full of garden gnomes with their little legs dangling over speckled toadstools, holding fishing rods. Sasha reaches out to touch a tiny bulbous nose. They carry on, through the warm, damp greenhouses with their windows misted with condensation, and into the cooler, fresher aquatics section. Five long tanks, lined with heavy black plastic sheeting, house the carp. A shaft of dim, brackish light comes from an underwater bulb. Anna peers over. Flashes of muscular fish flick through the water. Their metallic colours – silver, orange, blue-black – are even more glorious against the starkness of their tank.

'They're beautiful,' says Sasha.

Anna searches for the husband to help, but can't find him. Eventually, she spots the woman, who is tending to the hanging baskets. The woman sighs with irritation, steps down from her ladder, follows Anna back towards the aquatics department.

Sasha picks out two of the black carp, mottled with orange.

'These ones are more expensive,' the woman says. 'They're rarer, more prized.'

'How prized?' Anna asks.

'Twenty pounds more per fish.'

The price doesn't change her mind. Next, Isabella points to a silver variety. She likes them too. Anna asks for three of these. The woman prepares the packaging: a plastic bag filled with water from the tank resting within a stiff cardboard box to keep it upright. Sasha leans over the tank, watching as the woman slips a large net through the water, pulling in exactly the fish Anna requests. The girls become excited, pointing out other fish they'd like the woman to catch until she stops and puts down her net. 'That's ten fish,' she says. 'How big is your pond?'

When the fish are packaged, the woman leads Anna through to another department, suggesting waders, rubber gloves, strong secateurs. Anna will need to manage the greenery within the pond if the fish are to survive this time. It's more complicated – and far more expensive – than she had anticipated. Is it too late to cancel her project? Throw the fish back? Buy a goldfish instead? But the girls are excited. They're happy to be bringing back to life their mother's pond, and Anna can't bring herself to disappoint them.

At the till, Anna hands over her credit card. 'Don't throw the fish straight in the pond,' says the woman. 'Put the bags on top of the water and let them acclimatise. A quick temperature change might kill them. And we don't do refunds.'

The woman helps her out to the car with the boxes. They drive home with the faint thudding sound as the fish navigate their tiny temporary home.

'Thank you,' says Isabella.

'Yes,' says Sasha. 'Thank you.'

'We'll get them straight in, when we get home,' replies Anna.

They pass fields, turn left on to the back road, and keep driving on in silence until Isabella asks: 'Who *is* Brendan?'

Anna hesitates.

'Like, how do you know him?' she says.

Anna glances into the backseat through the rear-view mirror. Both girls are sitting up, their eyes flickering back and forth in silent communication.

'He's someone David and I have known for very many years. Why do you ask?'

Isabella shrugs. Anna can see that Sasha is focused, expectant, waiting for Isabella to drop a bomb.

'Go on,' says Anna. 'It's OK. You can tell me.'

'He's creepy,' says Sasha, eventually.

'Creepy?' asks Anna.

'He came into our room,' Isabella says.

'He did?' Anna says.

'Yeah. Knocked on the door and came straight in,' says Isabella.

'And started asking us questions,' adds Sasha.

'What kind of questions?'

'What we liked doing, how old we were. He picked up our stuff, sat on the bed,' says Sasha.

'Can you tell him not to do it again?' says Isabella.

'I'll talk to him,' replies Anna.

'Tell him not to just come in again, like he's known us for years,' says Isabella.

'He should have known better,' says Anna.

The girls say nothing.

'I'm sorry,' Anna says. 'I'm sorry he did that.'

'We wouldn't have minded Uncle David doing it,' says Sasha.

'Of course you wouldn't,' says Anna.

'Just not Brendan.'

'I'll tell him,' says Anna. 'Don't worry. He won't come in again.'

Anna stops at the top of the driveway to the house, types out a text message to David: *Brendan's been going into the girls' room. Can you talk to him???* She puts her phone away, then carries on down the drive to the house, where the girls remove the boxes of fish from the car. One each, they carry them out to the pond, holding them like precious objects, fearful of swishing them around, scaring the fish. At the pond, they place the boxes on the ground, take out the bagged fish, rest them on the water. Without thinking, they let them go. Bubbles of clear plastic, the young carp within, drift into the middle of the pond. Anna tries to reach them with the net, but they have travelled too far. She pulls on the waders to see if she can reach them that way, but long before she's anywhere near the fish, the water starts to spill over the top of the waders. She wades back to the side of the pond. The fish still bob along the surface of the water. She pulls off the boots, rolls her socks away.

'No choice,' says Anna.

She peels down her trousers, dips her toe into the cold, brown water. If only she'd never bought the bloody fish. Her feet sink into the bottom of the pond as she steps out. Cold, wet mud slips between her toes. The girls watch from the side of the water while Anna keeps moving towards the fish. Eventually, she catches the plastic bubbles, snips the top from each of them, gently submerging the fish into their new home. In an instant, they have disappeared into the depths. She wades back to the bank. Out of the water, she shakes with cold. Her skin is mottled blue; she's wet through. Her teeth chatter. She feels sick. She asks the girls to pour in the bucket of water treatment product while she runs inside, holding her clothes, to have a hot bath.

Their plans for a walk up the hill are aborted. It's raining again. Instead, the girls stay on the sofa, wrapped around each other like puppies, reading. David phones to say the boats have stopped running because of the high winds. He'll stay over in the pub with Brendan, return first thing the next morning. At bedtime, the wind still hasn't stopped. Anna checks on the girls, closes the shutters to stop the windows rattling, draws the curtains, tells them not to worry; it's only wind and rain. A shaft of silver moonlight has found its way through a crack in the shutters, creating a dart of light on the floor. Anna leaves the door open. They tell her they're used to weather like this. A little rain doesn't scare them. So Anna kisses them good night, goes to her own room.

She falls asleep to the sound of the wind battering the landscape. Doors bang. Rain hammers the glass. But it's a gentler sound that wakes her in the middle of the night. Whimpering, floating through the air like soft, pink paper. Anna sits up in bed, looks at her watch. She's only been asleep for two hours. She pulls herself out of bed, stepping from the warmth of the covers into the chill of the bedroom. Her face screwed up against the light, she searches for her sweater, a pair of slippers, then feels her way along the dark corridor towards the sound. Inside the bedroom, the shutters are open, and Isabella is sitting on the floor, facing the window, hugging her knees. The curtains are flying perpendicular to the ground.

'You'll make yourself ill,' Anna says, moving towards Isabella. 'What on earth are you doing?'

She throws a blanket around the girl, guides her away from the open window towards the bed, then wraps her in the covers, but still Isabella's teeth chatter. Anna rubs her shoulders, trying to create some heat.

'You mustn't harm yourself like that,' Anna says. 'You mustn't stand in front of an open window in the cold.'

Isabella looks so frail. Pale and clammy, with deep, grey rings around her eyes.

The shutters bang against the wall. Anna pulls at the windows to close them, but they're stiff, impossible to budge. Her feet struggle to grip the floor where the rain has been blown inside. She slips around, then grabs the curtain to stop herself from falling over altogether, but manages to pull the whole thing down. The curtain pole hangs at an angle, the green silk curtains lopsided, trailing the floor.

Eventually, Anna gets the window closed, the shutters across. Sasha is rolled into a ball on the corner of the bed, her head tucked into her knees, arms drawn around her, the damp sheets tangled beside. Anna strokes her hair, coaxes her to lie down. Sasha is cold. She says she wishes Isabella hadn't opened the window, but Isabella wouldn't listen. Isabella always does whatever she wants. She never listens to anyone else. She doesn't care about hurting people. Anna wraps a duvet around Sasha, tells her that Isabella is upset. She's not thinking as she normally would. 'But she's always like that,' says Sasha.

'I'm going to fetch you both something to warm you up,' Anna says.

In the kitchen, Anna boils the kettle, makes chamomile tea. When it's brewed, she stirs in a teaspoon of honey, pours it out into two china teacups. Upstairs, she gives one cup to Sasha, then props Isabella up with pillows so she can hand her the tea, but Isabella doesn't take it. She's sweating. Her cheeks are red. The pace of her breathing has quickened. She pulls the covers from Isabella, attempts to cool her.

'Leave me alone,' Isabella shouts.

'What is it, Isabella? Are you in pain?' asks Anna.

'No one cares if I'm here or not,' she replies.

'Of course I do,' says Anna. 'And David, too. We all care.'

'You don't,' Isabella says emphatically.

Her body heaves with the shallow breaths she manages to take. Her eyes are distant, unfocused. Anna presses her hand to Isabella's forehead. She's still hot. Anna feels helpless, inadequate. 'Breathe, Isabella. Just breathe.'

Isabella is sweating and shaking. Anna tries to mop her face, but she wrestles herself away, twisting and bending so no one can touch her. Her face is covered with tiny pellets of sweat. Sasha has crawled over to her on the bed. 'Isabella,' she whispers. 'Bella. Bella. Can you hear me?'

Anna whispers as well, reassuring her. She rests a hand on Isabella's chest. 'Breathe,' she says. 'Breathe, Isabella.' Her hand seems so large against the child's pale, sweating chest, as it rises and falls in jerks. 'It's a panic attack. You're not going to die. Breathe.' The pace of Isabella's breathing slows. 'You're safe,' Anna keeps saying, until finally Isabella's breathing is normal once again. Anna goes in closer still, takes the girl in her arms. Then she helps her to lie down, pulls the sheets around her. Sasha settles in next to her sister. 'It's four in the morning,' Anna says. 'Sleep. Let's sleep.'

In her own room, Anna lies back in her bed, wide awake now. She feels guilty, inadequate. There is no one who loves these girls in that urgent, observant way that a mother usually loves her children. She's failing at this. And she can't get warm. The sheets feel cold and stiff. Her ears are numb. The radiators are doing nothing. In the background, the house creaks. The wind slips through the cracks in the window frame. It's not a home, it's a symbiosis; nature enters the house and does as it pleases. The windows are black, but when she switches off the bedside lamp, the darkness of the bedroom changes the view. The sky comes alive, smeared with tiny white dots of light. The moon is a luminous disc thrown against this mass of light and dark. Anna tries to fathom this endless space. How long does it go on for? How far, deep, wide? What does it mean? What does sky that goes on forever mean? The light she sees began its journey to earth hundreds, thousands, of years ago. Light begun long before she was born – and the light leaving the stars now will not hit earth until long after she's gone. She can't bear this. She gets out of bed, stands at the window wrapped in a duvet. Anna pulls the blanket closer around herself. Human suffering is no greater than any other suffering. It has no consequence, no purpose. It's simply sorrow. It's not transformative, or redemptive as Brendan hopes. It's sorrow, and it won't do anything for you. It will arrive, then it will pass, leaving you no better or worse. There is no reward. It's the shifting ebb of life and death, the flow of human beings on and off the planet, of all beings on and off the planet. It means nothing. Outside, the sea foams, the wind rushes through the trees. The two girls are tormented, and within this huge expanse of sky, this torment is nothing more than a squirrel fleeing up a tree or a rabbit burrowing a hole. No ripple. Just two girls, small as ants. The moon and stars look down dispassionately. Anna is angry with David. She longs for the warmth of her own home in London – a house where you can't see the sky, you see only the life in front of you – where she feels none of these things. In London, you can't see all this blankness, all this emptiness. You see human endeavour, human connection. Anna longs for that life within a measurable, definable world.

All night, the wind continues to moan, the windows

shake. When morning comes, Anna awakes to a house bathed in calm. She has slept deeply, a dream-filled sleep, scattered with small mini-dreams: being in a shop, walking through fields, finding a sock in the earth which she pulls, and it keeps coming, an enormous, long sock in candy-coloured stripes that she pulls and pulls, never ending; she keeps dragging it up from the earth.

Anna checks in on the girls. Asleep. Outside, the intensity of the devastation becomes clear. Broken trees, grass littered with roof tiles, a telegraph pole in the distance leaning at a dangerous angle. A wisteria plant hangs away from the brick wall it was growing up. Anna picks up the tiles, sets the garden furniture upright, but nature must do the rest. By the pond, a tree has fallen, and there it must stay. These are jobs for someone else, for when she is gone. For now, they have enough to do.

The pond has been churned up into thin, liquid mud. Light reflects on the droplets of rain speckling the grass and plants, making them sparkle. The morning grows in intensity. Haze gives way to a crisp blue sky. Without warning, Anna feels herself well up with tears, because later she will go upstairs, pull the sheets from the bed, wash away the sweat of the night before, dry them, return them to the bed, knowing that the same drama will play itself out again, and again she will wash the bed so that the girls don't descend into complete chaos and squalor. Never before has she been confronted with her own helplessness, her own ineffectiveness. Whatever she does, all this will continue.

Inside, she picks up the phone to find out when David will return. No ringtone. She hits the receiver button, listens, but nothing. She hits it again, and again, and again. Still nothing. She crouches down to check the socket. It's intact. She pulls it out, re-inserts it. Still nothing. She tries the phone in the kitchen. Also dead. The library. Nothing. Upstairs, she checks in Rachel and Peter's bedroom. No sound. She goes through the house, lifting every receiver, hammering at the receiver button. Not a single phone is working. She sits down in an armchair and bursts into tears.

It's after midday before the girls get up. Wearing crumpled T-shirts and tracksuit trousers, long hair straggling down their backs, they look sleepy. When they arrive at the bottom of the stairs, Anna asks them how they are feeling.

'My stomach still hurts,' says Isabella.

Sasha pulls up a chair, reaches across the table for some orange juice.

'Where is the pain?' Anna asks.

'Everywhere,' replies Isabella.

'Please go upstairs and get dressed. I'm taking you to see a doctor.'

'Antidepressants?' says Brendan.

'Yes,' says Anna. 'The girls are suffering from depression.'

'No, they're sad,' says Brendan. 'Unsurprisingly.'

'But it's not passing. It's been going on for three months. There's plenty of help available if we just phone up and ask for it.' Anna slaps down a handful of leaflets she picked up at the doctor's surgery, for day centres, advice lines, mental health charities.

Brendan holds up his hand to Anna. 'They don't need medicating.'

'The doctor said there are plenty of techniques the girls can learn to help them manage.'

'Techniques?' Brendan says.

'There are plenty of qualified professionals who know how to handle this situation.'

'I know how to handle it,' says Brendan.

'What is this retreat from the world supposed to be achieving?' shouts Anna.

David looks startled. Anna is surprised by her own sudden outburst. She has no idea where this anger came from. It didn't even announce itself to her. Mild irritation, yes, but not this sudden force.

'You're being too hard on them,' David says.

'I am the person to help,' says Brendan. 'It's very important that we get this right.'

'But Brendan,' says Anna 'they're young girls, not case studies. You don't understand all this. You've never had children of your own. You can't just take over.'

Anna puts Granny Smith apples in a glass bowl, fills a jug of water. 'I'm taking these to the girls,' she says.

Upstairs, Anna finds Isabella and Sasha reading on their bed. She leaves the apples and the water. On her way out, she notices a small leak coming through the ceiling. Just a few drops sliding down a wall that is already stained brown. Anna wipes down the damp wall, and all the time she is cleaning, she is thinking, working up her indignation, until eventually she needs to find Brendan.

'I know you went into their room,' she snaps at him.

'I didn't; I've been through this with David. They're lying. I didn't. I didn't go in there,' he says.

'They say you did,' says Anna.

'Girls can be very self-conscious at that age,' Brendan says. He remains smooth, glib, unmoved by Anna's fury.

'Brendan, you can't wander into teenage girls' bedrooms. It's not on. They're girls, and you're a middle-aged man.'

But still, Brendan stays calm. He won't be drawn into Anna's fight, which makes her want to punch him even more. 'They were playing with me, Anna.' His gaze meets hers. Glassy blue eyes lined with dark lashes. His hair, with its sheen of chestnut, hangs thickly around his face, his curved mouth pushing downwards at the edges, giving him an expression of vulnerability, making him forlorn. 'They're setting me up,' Brendan whispers. 'And no one believes me.'

'They're just children,' replies Anna.

'I didn't do anything wrong.'

'Oh, let's just forget about it,' says Anna, but before she leaves, she turns to him, says very firmly: 'Just don't do it again.'

* * *

A few days later, Anna wanders into the library before anyone else is up. She wants to find a book to read, but is halted by the sight of the hearth. Candles, twenty of them, maybe more, stuck to the marble and burned down to their stubs. The remains of incense sticks sprout from wooden holders, worms of beige ash still intact beneath them. In the fireplace, the semi-burned remains of books. Anna wakes David to show him the scene.

'We were only singing,' he replies.

'You were there?'

'We lit some candles, listened to music, sang a little.'

'Ah,' says Brendan, entering the room. 'You found our lovely sing-song. It was fun, Anna. Anyway, I've been thinking about our conversation. Isabella isn't depressed. She's involved in a kind of purging. I've read about it countless times. Certain Native American tribes did a similar thing. They'd eat certain foods to bring on sickness to expel bad spirits.'

'Bad spirits?' says Anna.

'Our minds and bodies are far more complex than we can ever understand. In fact, David and I have been discussing another idea. We'd like to build a shrine.'

'A shrine?' says Anna.

'Yes. A shrine. David and I thought we should put it down by the river, away from the house. A place they are happiest, by the water, bringing back memories of summer, of warmer times.'

Anna stays silent.

'And it gives everyone something to do, a purpose. We can spend our days building them a shrine – and they can help. They'll have a project. You wanted a project for them, Anna.'

'A shrine?' Anna says again.

'A shrine,' says Brendan firmly. 'A shrine for them to worship at. To heal them. We discussed it with the girls last night, and the idea makes them happy. They also thought building it by the sea would be the best place.'

'It's a mad idea,' says Anna.

'It's doesn't have to just be about remembering. Shrines can be to forget too.'

'I liked Rachel – loved her, even. Still, does she need to be enshrined? Peter too?'

'It's for the girls,' David says.

'Peter would hate it.'

'You don't know that, Anna,' says David.

'We need to do something for those of us left behind,' says Brendan. 'It's not relevant to try and work out what Peter might have thought.'

'If they were adults,' Anna says, 'I would say yes, sure, build a shrine, if that's what you want to spend your days doing. But the girls are young – too young for this. They need life framing for them. They are immature, emotionally. They need protecting. It isn't good to wander aimlessly along this internal trail of sadness and pain. It's too much for girls of this age. They need us to make sense of this experience for them, not heighten it.'

'We're protecting them,' says Brendan.

'Not from their imaginations, you're not.'

'We're helping them – helping them to be free of their sadness.'

'What will it achieve?'

'I'm using my sabbatical to help you and David, Anna.'

'I just,' says Anna, softening her stance, 'I just don't believe that we need to depart too dramatically from the sobriety of traditional Western grieving.'

Brendan begins a retort to Anna, but before the words can come out, Anna has another idea: 'What about cork boards for the girls' bedroom that they could pin memories to? Or they can buy carved wooden boxes and then each girl could keep things inside: pieces of jewellery, cards, letters, items of clothing. Wherever they go, they can take these treasures with them. Then, when they need to, they can open them and be comforted. This way, they'll still be free. One day, the house will have to be cleared and its future thought about: these boxes could help them transition.'

'Anna, keep your voice down. No one is talking about moving,' David snaps.

'But David . . .'

'The girls mustn't hear the barest hint they might have to leave,' says David.

'But I thought the whole point of us being here is to help them transition to a life in London. We haven't made the right arrangements to be up here indefinitely. What about the cat?'

'Not yet, Anna. You're rushing.'

'Whoever ends up buying this house will just knock their shrine down. They're not going to care about the feelings of two girls. It'll be another loss.'

'Anna!' shouts David. 'You're being insensitive.'

But all Anna can think of is the time when those two girls will have to be prised out of the house like the slippery flesh from two oysters. They'll be upset, because they love the house – but it will have to happen. Anna's not being cruel, she's being practical. A shrine is the last thing they need.

'I've thought about all this. I think a shrine will be a wonderful project,' says Brendan. 'I have a design in mind, but it's not just what it will look like. We need to think about its purpose. Is it a thing of beauty, a monument to admire, or a place the girls can use? Joyful or sombre? Clad in untreated wood and left to go silver with age, or bold and bright, happy, to cheer them up?'

'Peter would hate it,' Anna says again.

'He might be happy to see the girls occupied, seeming brighter,' says David.

'No parent would want their children to build a shrine to them.'

'I don't agree with you, Anna,' says David.

'They're vulnerable young girls. They're not case studies for Brendan's next paper,' Anna says.

Anna needs some air. She wants a walk. David says he'll go with her. Even though the weather is terrible – the wind is blowing her sideways – Anna wants to be away from the house, from the girls, from Brendan. She's beginning to resent Brendan more deeply than she ever thought she would. His overzealousness, his insistence that he knows best, his demand to be in control. And the business of going into the girls' bedroom. Each side was so convincing, yet someone must be lying.

'I'm worried for the girls,' says Anna. 'They're at that age where they're persuadable. And Brendan is very persuasive.'

'I think the girls are doing well,' says David.

'But where will it all end?' asks Anna.

They walk through a tunnel of bare laburnum, emerge into a wood that runs parallel with the shore. The branches of the trees meet across the path, forming a thick canopy. Clean air gives way to a damp mushroom smell.

'Brendan's fun for the girls,' says David.

'But his ideas,' says Anna. 'He's so preachy and cack-handed. When was anything authentic? It's so pious. He's unstable. And it's worrying for the girls. They're easily led. Where he's planning on leading them?'

They follow a path made of compacted earth deep into the woods, then cross back over towards the shoreline. They pick their way around obstacles, jumping over craggy rock pools. David is distant, not himself. Anna is beginning to worry.

'You can talk to me,' Anna says.

'I know,' he replies.

On their way back towards the house, they make a detour to the pond to feed the fish. The smooth black water reflects the sky. Bright white cumulus clouds drift across the surface. The plump, shiny leaves of *Fatsia japonica* plants cocoon the water. Anna loves this enclosed little haven. David sits on the pontoon. Anna throws a fistful of pellets into the water. The muscular bodies of the carp pound the surface of the water each time the pellets rain down, shattering the image of the clouds. When the fish stop eating, disappear back underneath the water, the surface goes still. Once again, the clouds are reflected perfectly. She scatters more food, breaking the surface into millions of tiny, vibrating fragments. The fish eat. They disappear. The water is still. The clouds return.

'I understand the need to memorialise Rachel and Peter,' says Anna. 'But a shrine? A few objects are all they need.'

'Brendan's convinced about the shrine,' says David.

By the time they arrive back at the house, the girls are awake and in the library with Brendan. Three purple yoga mats are rolled out. Each of them is standing on one leg, their arms stretched above their heads, hands touching in prayer position.

'And breathe in, one . . . two . . . three . . .' Brendan instructs.

Their eyes closed, the girls' nostrils suck in as they take deep, full breaths.

'And out, one . . . two . . . three . . .' Brendan continues.

The girls blow out, then lower their hands. They follow

113

Brendan's next move. He wants them to let their arms stay straight, hovering away from their bodies, palms facing forward. 'And breathe in, one . . . two . . . three . . .'

'Are you sure this is right?' says Sasha, opening her eyes to check in with Brendan. She meets his gaze examining her.

'Almost.'

He takes her hands in his, moves them slightly behind her back. 'Can you feel that?'

'Yes,' says Sasha.

'It should feel lovely in the shoulders.'

'Yes,' says Sasha. 'I can feel them stretching. It *is* nice.'

'Can you do the same to me?' says Isabella eagerly, her eyes snapping open to see what she is missing out on.

Brendan stands in front of Isabella, examines the position of her arms, then gently pushes them slightly behind her.

'Good?' he asks.

'Can't really feel it,' says Isabella.

'Perhaps try and clasp your hands behind your back, if you're more flexible.' He takes Isabella's hands, moves them further behind her, attempts to push her hands together.

'Ouch!' she says, jumping away from him.

'Just go the way you were before. It'll be fine,' he says, returning to his mat.

'You're not joining in, David?' says Brendan, looking over to Anna and David.

'I'm giving it a miss,' David replies.

'It would do you good,' says Brendan.

'Yoga's not my thing,' says David. 'Definitely not.'

In the sitting room, Brendan pushes up the sleeves of his military green sweater. At the base of his chair, the girls sit with their legs curled beneath them, leaning against it. Sasha has a bright pink scarf tied around her head like a band, which she keeps untying, gathering the hair away from her face, then re-tying into a double knot.

Isabella plays with a large piece of red plasticine, twisting it into a corkscrew shape until it is almost as thin as hair. Sasha watches her, not irritated, but at least aware, it seems, that her sister has taken the entire piece of modelling clay for herself. Brendan bought it for both of them. Isabella notices her sister's gaze, pulls the clay into two pieces, hands half of it, with a sigh, to Sasha. Sasha idly rolls it into a ball, flattens it, rolls it again. Wordlessly, they pass it between them, shaping it, destroying it, shaping it again. Anna's transfixed by the girls, by the quiet, efficient way they communicate together, by their desire to break the thing they've made the moment it's completed. Isabella moulds the shape of a leaf, picks up a teaspoon and draws lines for the leaf's veins, then immediately scrunches it up.

'That leaf was lovely,' says Anna. 'Why did you ruin it?'

Isabella shrugs, retreats into herself. After a moment, she turns to Brendan and says: 'We should build the shrine near the silver birches. They're my favourite trees.'

'It's the smell of the sea I love,' says Sasha. 'As soon as I smell the sea, I know I'm home.'

Brendan takes the pieces of clay from the girls, rolls a small piece of it into a tiny sphere. The rest, he shapes and pinches into a solid cube that he places in the middle of the table. He holds the sphere between thumb and forefinger. 'This is the sun. It will start here in the morning, and move like this,' he says, taking the piece from the front of the cube to the back. 'If we get the light right, the shrine will awaken something within you.'

'Oh,' says Isabella. 'Well, I don't care about that. All I want is a place to put my photos.'

'No,' he says. 'I'll take you down to show you.'

Brendan fetches David, and the four of them walk to the shore to see where they might build a shrine. From the window, Anna watches them. They stand by the edge of the sea. Overhead, birds make white darts against the cloudless sky. It's late afternoon, and the sun is slung low. Its muted light gathers around the trees' bare branches, coating the wood so that together they manage to make solid light. The landscape glistens. The four of them – David, Brendan and the two girls – stand in a line, their heads tilted upwards, watching the birds. The girls run through the wet grass, their hands trailing behind them. The wind is up again, so the sea foams against the shore. The four of them gaze out at the water, holding hands. The wind slips up inside Brendan's jacket, forcing it outwards like a balloon. They stand like that until Sasha breaks from

116

the group, flings her arms out to catch the wind, letting it blow her to an angle, almost knocking her over. Then Isabella breaks away, too, runs after a red bucket that the wind has sent skidding across the field. When it starts to rain, they come into the kitchen, shaking the water from their coats, telling Anna they've found the place they want to build.

digging

THE CORNERS OF THE KITCHEN WINDOWS ARE MISTED WITH
condensation. Outside, the bare branches of the trees are
covered in ice, turning them into white sculptures that fan
out over the chilly black water. The girls crunch through
the frozen grass towards the shore. Ahead of them, Brendan
and David let out spurts of hot breath that solidify into
smoke: a pair of old steam trains puffing towards the sea.
As she walks, Sasha looks down at her feet to examine the
way her footsteps crush the grass made brittle with frost.
Underneath their coats, both girls are still wearing nighties.
Their blue wellies don't quite cover their calves, leaving a
few inches of bare skin exposed. Both children feel their
bodies constrict with the cold, regret being rushed out of
the door by Brendan. They wish they'd listened to Anna,
who'd urged them to take their time, to dress properly.

'Come on,' Sasha says. 'Let's catch up with David and
Brendan.'

The girls' boots slap against their bare legs as they break

into a run. At the water's edge, Brendan is leaning on his spade, surveying the area.

'You didn't wait for us,' Sasha says, catching her breath.

But Brendan is not listening. He's searching through his box of supplies for pegs, string, a tape measure, two brand-new stainless-steel trowels.

'We bought these for you,' says David, handing one each to the girls. They begin picking off the sticky labels, proud to have their own tools. While they do this, Brendan and David mark out a rectangle with string. They work quickly, using their feet to push in the pegs, then wrapping the red string tightly around these pegs, connecting each one to the next, until they have the shape of their base. They start together at the corner closest to the sea, using all their weight to plunge the spades as far into the ground as they'll go, pulling out large clods of soil, which they toss on to a heap behind them.

'You start over there, girls,' says Brendan, pointing to the opposite corner. Crouching beside one another, they begin scratching at the earth with their shiny new trowels. They may as well be digging with teaspoons, but they carry on, unsure what their purpose is in all of this. If they keep worrying away at it – scraping with their bare hands when they have to – they will make a hole, and this, they understand, will be useful.

After an hour crouched like this, their bare knees are covered in mud, the skin on their legs is red with cold, their noses are running, their hands are black, and still they've barely made an indent in the earth. This is pointless. To the other side, the men are leaping ahead, already digging a second hole. Sasha stops work, throws down her stupid little spade. Useless thing, anyway. She wants to go home to fetch some warm things for them both. Why did Brendan rush them out of the door, anyway? Anyone would think it was his shrine, not theirs. But just as she's about to leave, she spots Anna heading towards them with a bag hanging over her shoulder.

'You're freezing,' she says. 'You can't work like this. What are those two thinking?' Anna's warm palms envelop Sasha's cold hands. 'Come on, both of you,' says Anna. She hands them each a pair of long woollen socks, then a hat, a thick sweater and finally a pair of blue woollen gloves. Next, Anna pours hot chocolate from a flask into two tin mugs. The girls gulp it down, cupping their hands around the hot metal to help stop their shivering. When they finish, Anna screws the lid back on the flask, while reminding them that they can always come home. 'You don't have to do everything you're told,' she says, nodding towards Brendan and David.

Sasha's eyes follow Anna back to the house, then she looks down at the cold pit of earth in front of her. It might feel simpler to be indoors with Anna, pottering about in the warm. Does she really want to build this thing? But she's been told that she must. It will be good for her. It's for her mum and dad, so she must try her hardest. She carries on digging because she doesn't want to disappoint anyone.

Crouched at their little hole again, knees hurting, back aching, nothing but determination – she mustn't fail – she keeps going. When she looks over, the men have very nearly finished digging their second hole and it makes her feel, once again, as if this whole thing is pointless.

'This is unfair,' protests Isabella. 'We could have just as big a hole as you two if we had proper spades.'

'OK!' says Brendan. 'Let's swap!'

The two men give the girls their spades in exchange for the trowels. Now the men are crouching and the girls are jumping on to the edges of the spades, feeling them easily slice through the earth.

'See!' says Isabella.

But it's hard work. The girls are quickly out of breath, and, eventually, even these spades are boring. The whole thing is boring. Manual labour: who in their right mind would do that? Isabella thought making a shrine would mean framing photographs, planting seeds, thinking about which relic to place where. Not this. She throws down her spade in protest. Sasha does the same. They're tired, they need a break.

'Take one, then,' says Brendan.

The girls tour the edge of the shrine, inspecting the large, square holes already dug by Brendan and David. They jump over the string marker, like hopscotch, going from one side to the other. Sasha checks that the men are watching – they are – so she carries on bouncing flirtatiously across the line, giggling, she and Isabella slapping each

121

other's hands as they pass one another. Then Isabella jumps down into one of the holes, disappears into it, then scrambles up the other side and out. The pristine square collapses inwards, but she doesn't care. Sasha jumps down too, spoiling the hole even more. They do one more lap of the string, before falling on to the ground, panting.

David sighs. He patiently fixes the mess while Brendan takes the girls' hands, pulls them upright. He brushes undergrowth from the backs of their coats: what naughty girls they are. They must start behaving. The girls giggle again.

'Perhaps it's time to stop work for the day,' says David.

They head back to find Anna at the door waiting for them. Small sausages of mud come loose from the ridges of their boots, scatter like animal droppings. Sasha holds on to the wall, raises a leg. Anna pulls off the dirty wellies, then scoots around with a dustpan and brush to take up the mess. While she cleans, Brendan reports: he's thrilled with the girls; they've thrown themselves into the building; they haven't been afraid of hard work or getting their hands dirty; they've toiled through cold, through hunger, through moments of doubt. Brendan puts his arm around Sasha – the onion smell of sweat – and kisses her on the cheek, tells her he's proud of her, and she wonders why he's lying. She wriggles away from him, gulps down a glass of orange juice, pours one for her sister, then they run upstairs to wash.

'What do you think of him?' Isabella asks, as she stands beside her sister in the old enamel bath.

'He smells a bit,' replies Sasha.

'He does, doesn't he? I noticed that! B.O.'

'And shit,' says Sasha.

'No! That's gross.'

'I bet he doesn't wash.'

'He must wash sometimes,' says Isabella.

'He's hairy and smelly, like a dog.'

'Let's go into his room.'

Sasha's eyes widen. 'Yes,' she whispers. 'Let's.'

'I'll check he's not coming.'

Isabella runs off along the landing to the top of the stairs, where she listens out. Brendan is deep in conversation with David about shrines and memory, about why we need to build at times like this. She runs back. Slowly, they open the door and peek around it. Brendan's room is impeccably neat. They hadn't expected that. A brown leather suitcase is open on the floor. Inside, a few white T-shirts, carefully folded. In the corner of the room, there's a cupboard, which Sasha looks inside to find shirts, a brown jacket, white underpants, all in a neat pile on the shelf above the hanging rails. Balled brown socks beside them. In the bottom of the cupboard, a beige washbag. Inside: herbal toothpaste, a bamboo toothbrush, a crystal deodorant and a square bar of olive oil soap.

Sasha pulls it out. 'Look! He does wash.'

'He's like a monk,' says Isabella.

She steps up on to the carefully made bed, leaps across it towards the bookstand on the other side, where her hand lands on a small bag of sherbet lemons. 'Will he notice?' says Isabella, letting her fingers wriggle inside the bag.

'Do monks eat sweets?' asks Sasha.

Isabella takes out two, keeping one for herself, putting the other into her sister's waiting hand. They pop them into their mouths, their saliva immediately activated by the sourness of the lemon flavour. They keep going through the room, sucking on the sweets as they open drawers, inspect the books on the nightstand, check underneath the bed.

'What a strange man he is,' says Isabella. 'What's he even doing here? Has he got any friends?'

'He's got Anna and David. They seem to like him.'

The girls lean up against his bed, still sucking on the sweets. Then they hear the hallway door open. Shot through with nerves, they run out of the room and down the corridor to their own bedroom, where they spit out the stolen sweets into their palms while they catch their breath.

The next morning, Brendan and David load up the trailer with rolls of plastic sheeting, wooden posts, and bags of sand, stones and cement. They attach it to Peter's tractor, which Brendan drives. The girls wedge themselves among this stuff. David walks alongside to keep an eye out for falling cargo. At the water's edge, they jump off the trailer. Taking an end each of a heavy roll of plastic, they wrestle it up on to their tiny shoulders, determined that they will work harder than they did the previous day: they're going to enjoy this. Together, they scurry off towards the shore like fastidious little worker ants. Back and forth they go, unloading bags of cement, metal buckets, stones. Brendan and David work, too, heaving bags of sand, throwing them down alongside the girls' spoils. The cement bags let out puffs of grey smoke as they land like magic tricks. The last one, carried by Brendan, splits open. He swears, gathers up the two ends to stop it splitting further, and then, crouched over and hobbling, he lays it gently next to the rest of the supplies.

When the trailer is empty, the girls are pleased with themselves. The men are pleased with them. They've done a good job. They worked hard without complaining. So Brendan gives them another job: to hold the wooden posts centrally within the holes while he hammers in the battens and pegs to keep them straight. They work in twos – David and Sasha, Isabella and Brendan. Afterwards, Brendan gives the girls a metal bucket each, sends them to the shore to fetch water while he makes the dry mix of stone, cement and sand on a large sheet of plastic.

At the water's edge, Sasha holds her bucket down against the pebbles, but doesn't gather anything. Too shallow. Every time she lifts her bucket, the tiny trickle of water flows straight out, so she steps out to deeper water – as far as she can go before it's too much for her boots – and this time she manages to fill the bucket. She runs back to Brendan with her prize. He empties it into his mixture, which David begins to stir with a long, wooden stick. It's not enough so Brendan sends her back for more. Like this, both girls go back and forth to the sea, fetching bucket after bucket of water, until Brendan finally tells them they can stop. He hands them each a stick and the four of them stand around the plastic sheet, mixing the concrete. When that's done, Brendan and David layer stones into the base of one of the holes, pouring the concrete over while the girls make sure the wooden posts don't move.

All morning, they work like this, only taking a break when Anna arrives with some sandwiches for lunch. They eat quickly, then get back to work, doing the same job over and over again. Fetching water, mixing concrete, setting each wooden post within its foundations. They keep working until the fading light forces them to stop.

'And now,' Brendan says, 'we should christen it.'

He fetches another bucket of water and takes two torches from his pocket, which he places on the ground, arranging them so they point upwards. The two beams of light are set at angles either side of the square of concrete, intersecting to form an X-shape that illuminates the branches of the trees overhead. Through those bare branches, it's possible to catch glimpses of the sky: pale and chilly, stars, a sliver of moon, wisps of the Milky Way.

'Take off your socks and roll up your trousers,' instructs Brendan.

'What for?' says Isabella.

'Just do it,' he replies, impatiently.

Slowly, Isabella removes her socks, and folds the bottoms of her trousers upwards until her calves are exposed. Brendan asks her to stand. She's nervous, but David is there; at least she trusts him. Brendan asks her to hold on to his shoulders as he guides her foot towards the wet concrete, lowering it until he's able to press it into the surface. It squelches between her toes. She wants to let go, but Brendan's grip is firm around her ankle, and if she moves, she'll fall over, so she stays very still while he keeps her foot firmly in its place. Eventually though, he pulls it out, plunging it straight into the waiting bucket of seawater. She winces. It's freezing. He leaves her like that while he finds an upturned bucket for her to sit on. Then he uses a cloth to gently rub away the remains of the concrete from between her toes. When this is done, he takes her foot within the soft interior lining of his coat and pats it dry.

'There,' he says. 'All done.' He helps her put on her socks and boots again, then turns to Sasha. 'Now, it's you,' he says. On her, he performs the same ritual. The imprint, the washing, the drying, the putting on of socks and shoes.

Next, it's David's turn. When all three are done – he won't do his own foot, Brendan says, because it's not his memorial, he's just the conduit – they use the torches to admire their work. David's footprint looms over the two smaller ones, Isabella's marginally bigger than Sasha's, but all three are so detailed you can make out the lines of the skin like the veins on leaves. David has a thought: he reaches for a stick. Above each foot, he carefully scratches into the wet concrete their initials, followed by the date. *SH, IH, DH. 11/12/19.*

The next day, it rains, heavy rain sweeping off the sea, arriving on shore in thick, foggy folds. The girls are trapped inside. They're bored. They lie around, staring out of the window, twiddling the fabric of their T-shirts. The house feels like a prison. Anna gives them a pile of *National Geographic* magazines she'd found by Rachel's bed. Would they like to read them? They wouldn't. She suggests they help out in the house. They don't want to. Why is Anna so determined to occupy them? What's wrong with just lying around, doing nothing?

Later, when the rain calms to a drizzle, Sasha puts on her coat because she wants to go to the shrine. She examines their initials. Tiny letter-shaped ponds. Next to them, another shape. Sasha crouches to get a better look. It's a hoof print. A curious deer? A lost sheep? She runs her finger along the inside of it. It's already dried and hardened, become a little pond all of its own.

The wooden posts are wet through. Sasha wanders between them, an emptiness tugging within her. What's the point of these stalks of wood? Her eyes flicker over the bare trees, the wet earth, the house beyond full of strangers. The sea is as it always is. The trees have been standing for hundreds of years. Their height and their immovability feel like arrogance. They're taunting her, childishly proving that they have something she doesn't. They get to stay the same, whereas she's been forced into a new life. She gathers up rocks, stacks them in a pile, hurls them one after the other at the shrine, as hard as she can. The stalks of wood barely even shudder, if she manages to hit them at all. The concrete doesn't break. She gathers up all her strength, tries ever harder, but it is so solid, so surely its own thing, that it can easily withstand her. She hates it even more for that. She throws more and more, until a hand landing on her shoulder stops her.

Brendan gathers her up towards him. She doesn't want to be hugged, but he pulls her in anyway, until she stops resisting – it does feel nice. Her face rests against the coolness of his wax jacket, the chemical smell of the wax, then the scent of peppermint mixed with tobacco as he whispers to her that all will be fine in the end. His fingers comb through her hair. He twists it gently into a ponytail, lets it fall again, all the time whispering to her that she will find her way. After a while like this, he breaks away to fiddle with his wrist. He removes a plaited bracelet in red and white thread. Dangling from it, a small charm. 'An amulet,' he says. He rests it against the pad of his finger for Sasha to examine. Concentric star-shapes in gold, a red stone in the middle. He asks Sasha to hold out her wrist so he can tie it on, a double knot so it won't come off. 'Don't part with it,' he says. 'Ever. It'll keep you safe.'

Sasha holds up her wrist to admire the amulet dangling from the plaited thread. The white thread is dulled with dirt – Brendan's sweat? Yesterday's digging? – but the red thread is still shiny and new.

'Thank you,' she says. 'I like it.'

'It's made of silk,' replies Brendan. 'So it's very strong. It'll never come off.'

Together, they walk back to the house, where Anna has already put the food out on the table. Sasha goes upstairs to change out of her wet clothes. The bedroom is clean, because Anna has been in, folding and tidying. The drawers are full of freshly laundered things. She puts on clean, dry clothes, goes back downstairs for dinner, twisting the bracelet around her wrist.

It's morning. The light in the girls' bedroom has the sharpness and luminosity of light bouncing off snow. The sound of the sea and the bleating of the sheep are both muffled. The girls don't want to get out of bed. They'll stay here all day. Isabella pulls the duvet up to her chin. Sasha twists the amulet on her bracelet between thumb and forefinger.

'What's that?' asks Isabella.

'Brendan gave it to me.'

'Why?' her sister asks.

'I was upset yesterday,' says Sasha.

Isabella stays silent. She gets out of bed, puts on thick socks, a warm sweater, doesn't say anything more to her sister. She worked every bit as hard as Sasha on the shrine, was equally nice to Brendan. She would have liked a bracelet just as much, and she's annoyed not to have one.

Downstairs, she finds Anna buttering toast, making a pot of tea. When she sits, Anna offers her orange juice, fusses that the glasses aren't clean. Isabella becomes irritated with her. Why does everything have to be so precise? Why's she such a control freak? She hates it! Go away! Leave me alone! No, I don't have any laundry I need doing. No, I don't want anything more to eat. Isabella takes the glass of orange juice, a piece of toast, stomps into the sitting room to eat her breakfast in peace, ignoring Sasha who has come down and headed into the kitchen.

Isabella hears Brendan arrive back from his trip for supplies. He stamps snow from his feet, complains about the cold. 'I need a coffee,' he says. 'I skidded off the road. A patch of ice threw me into the verge. I had to rock the car back and forth to get it out. I had no gloves. It's freezing out there.'

'Poor you,' says Sasha.

While Brendan drinks his coffee, he sets out the plan for the day. He'll go down to the shrine ahead of everyone else, clear away the snow with a shovel and brush. He'll find something to light a fire in, an old grate or tractor wheel perhaps, to keep them all warm while they're building. Then, together, they'll start to construct the floor, build the walls. 'The shrine will really begin to take shape, girls,' he says. 'You'll both need to help hold up the planks so that David and I can secure them with nails.'

'Well . . . I don't want to do that,' says Isabella, coming into the kitchen.

Startled, Brendan turns to look.

'It's freezing. And I think that's a very boring job.

131

Standing in the cold, holding up wood.'

Brendan takes a deep breath in, ready to speak, but Isabella beats him to it: 'Daddy would never have expected me to be standing out in the freezing cold, holding up planks of wood. If this shrine is supposed to be in his memory, then you're not doing a very good job of it.'

Isabella marches out of the room. She expects someone to follow her – keeps checking behind her – but no one does. So, alone, she sits at her bedroom window, watching Brendan at the shrine as he sweeps away the snow, just as he said he would, positioning an iron grate close to where they will work. He builds a fire using newspaper, kindling, logs. When the fire takes hold, he returns to the house. Next, she sees Brendan, David and Sasha returning to the shrine. A happy little threesome. Isabella slumps off the bed to find Anna.

'I'm staying with you today,' she says.

'And what shall we do together?' Anna asks.

Isabella shrugs.

'We could make a cake?'

'How?'

'First we need a bowl,' says Anna.

Isabella fetches a bowl, returns to Anna's side.

'Next we need the ingredients. Butter, sugar, eggs, flour.'

Anna weighs out the ingredients, shows Isabella how to beat the butter and sugar together with a wooden spoon.

'This is fun,' says Isabella.

'You've never made a cake before?'

'Is that odd?'

'You didn't do this with your mum?'

'With her, we used to go kayaking, or camping on the beach. We'd build fires, catch fish. But no, nothing like this. She'd have found it boring. Please can I be the one to crack the eggs?'

Anna hands her the box of eggs. Isabella breaks them into the mix.

'Do you think we're weird?' she asks.

'Why would I think that?' says Anna.

While the mixture is in the oven, they sit at the table to wait. Isabella keeps checking through the glass to watch it rise, eventually turn golden. Anna fetches two plates and two forks, slices into the warm cake to give them both a piece.

'I'm sorry I've been so mean,' says Isabella.

'You haven't been mean,' replies Anna.

'I'm just so confused,' Isabella says.

But before Anna can answer, the door bursts open. Brendan, with Sasha behind him. 'We're taking you hostage, Isabella,' he says. He pulls Isabella's chair out from the table, flings her over his shoulder and runs out, chased by Sasha. Isabella squeals because the bone of his shoulder digs into her stomach. It hurts! She thumps him. Demands he put her down, but he refuses to until they're at the shrine, where he plonks her down in front of David.

'We won't have you sulking,' says Brendan. 'The shrine is for everyone.'

'I wasn't sulking,' mumbles Isabella.

'Oh, yes you were,' he says. She wants to thump him again.

They begin work, and over the course of the day, the shape of the shrine emerges as they fit more wood to the frame. Finally, by nightfall, it's a deep rectangle – an enormous wooden box – with what will be a small door at one corner. No windows – which both girls think is odd – but Brendan tells them he's going to buy a ladder. The roof is flat. They'll be able to climb up on to it if they want a view.

They follow Brendan into the shrine. He sweeps his torch around it. The girls' eyes flicker upwards around the ceiling, along the rough, splintered walls.

'It's cold in here,' Sasha says.

'It isn't meant to provide shelter,' says Brendan. 'Its purpose is to make you feel something.'

'I don't really get what it's *for*,' says Isabella.

'You don't like it?' he asks.

'No,' Sasha says, pacing the room. 'We do like it. We just need to get used to it.'

'We're just not sure what we're going to do in here,' replies Isabella.

'But that's what your imagination is for,' says Brendan. 'That's the whole fun of it.'

Isabella has to go sideways through the kitchen door to allow passage of the large cardboard box she's carrying.

Brendan stops her, tells her it's not a good idea to clutter the space. Isabella snaps back: it's her shrine. She'll do what she wants with it. Brendan tries again. It should be a calm space, where they can think, talk, reflect.

But Isabella is insistent. It's her space. She doesn't want emptiness and reflection. She wants fun and objects. He said they could use their imaginations, and she wants to put things in it: a straw hat of Rachel's. Peter's reading glasses. A box of photographs. A sketch of the sea her mother made. Brendan tries to tell her that the whole point of shrines is that they are about the spiritual, the non-physical – it's about feeling and nothing else – at which point Isabella yells at him: 'It's physical to me, so fuck off!' then storms out of the room, sobbing.

'Well done, Brendan,' says David.

'She's a child. Why won't she just do as she's told? I was only trying to help – my whole mission up here has been to help,' he says angrily, putting his arm around Sasha who stays very still in spite of wanting him to let go of her. She doesn't want to make him any angrier than he already is. 'But there are certain things that Isabella just isn't understanding. Filling the shrine up with a load of clutter from the past will distract their mission. They mustn't be gazing backwards; they must move beyond all this. They must press on forwards.'

'Is it really so important?' Anna asks. 'They're kids. It's only stuff.'

'Yes!' says Brendan, slamming his fist down on the table.

'It's not just a bit of fun. It's supposed to have a purpose.'

'You're being really unfair,' says Sasha, running off upstairs to find her sister. In their bedroom, she spots the lump in the bed. Sasha burrows under the duvet beside Isabella, pulls it back up over their heads. They lie very still. Cocooned in their bed, the girls feel safe from the adults. Under the covers, in the dark, they whisper. Their hot, tinny breath lands on each other as they speak, but they don't mind. They're used to each other's bodies. They fit together. When they interconnect, arms around each other's neck, legs resting in the other's lap, they feel as if they're one person, and like this, formed into a single being, they are whole enough to chase away anything the adults might bring to them. They'll stay like this, jumbled up under the covers, for as long as it takes to feel better.

They hear Brendan's voice: 'Hi, girls. Mind if I come in?'

They keep very still and very quiet, barely dare to breathe. Footsteps. They grip each other's hands. A blast of cold air. Light. The duvet is pulled back in a single, brutal tug: 'There you are!' he says. 'Why are you hiding?'

Brendan sits on the bed. Sasha pulls her pink-and-white striped nightie over her knees so that all that is visible of her is a head and two feet poking out, like a penguin.

'Look at you!' Brendan says, pinching the nightie between his thumb and forefinger. 'Don't you look cute! You're like a little stick of raspberry-flavoured candy cane. Sweet enough to lick. And you look lovely, too,' he says to Isabella.

Her lip curls. She looks away. He goes to touch her

nightie, but she rolls quickly out of his way, stands up. 'Don't touch me,' she snaps.

'Isabella,' he says.

Isabella says nothing.

'I have a feeling I know what the problem is . . . it's about . . . would you like to have one of my bracelets? I think you wanted one of my bracelets, too, and you're cross and jealous that I didn't give you one.'

Isabella will not answer him – cross and jealous? She feels like telling him to fuck off again – so Brendan starts to pull a thin, silver chain from his wrist. He rolls it over his hand, dangles it from his index finger in front of her like a temptation. As it moves, it catches the light. The silver sparkles. It is very pretty. Isabella doesn't move. She stands, looking at the piece of jewellery only through the corner of her eye, so that no one else can see her looking. But Brendan continues to hold the bracelet in front of her, swinging it in the light, undeterred. From the chain hangs a small purple stone encircled in silver.

'Is that an amethyst?' Isabella eventually asks.

'It is,' says Brendan. 'Isn't it lovely?'

Isabella touches the stone, flicks it lightly, admires the way it moves.

'Here,' says Brendan. 'Hold out your hand.'

Reluctantly, she raises her hand, allowing Brendan to slip the bracelet over her fingers, up her palm and on to her wrist, where he fiddles with the chain, tightening it so it won't fall off.

'It wasn't right of me to give Sasha a bracelet and not you,' he says.

'I don't really care,' says Isabella. She gazes intently at Brendan, but doesn't say anything, then drops her hand to her waist, hoping that he doesn't notice how pleased she is to finally have a bracelet too.

'Do you like it?' Brendan asks.

'It's OK,' she says.

Brendan's gaze shifts towards the window. 'Oh look, you can see the shrine from here.'

'On a clear day, we can see the neighbouring islands,' says Sasha.

'Lucky you! I can't see a thing from the pokey little room Anna put me in,' says Brendan.

'That was mean of her,' says Sasha.

'It's OK,' he says. 'I'm surviving.'

'I can talk to her,' says Sasha. 'It's our house. You can sleep wherever you like.'

But Brendan doesn't respond. Instead, he kisses each girl lightly on the cheek, tells them both to get dressed – there's work to be done on the shrine – then leaves the room. When he's gone, Isabella touches her bracelet, rolling it around her wrist, looking more closely at the small, purple stone.

Sasha glances over, her eye flickering jealously over her sister's chain. Her own bracelet, only made from thread, seems less special compared to the sparkle of the silver one.

'You'll have to be careful with that,' says Sasha. 'It's a

very fine chain, and could easily break. Mine is made of silk, so it's very strong.'

In front of the mirror, Sasha stands in her nightie. She holds the sides of it, teasing them outwards so the skirt makes a fan shape. Her eyes flicker up and down the length of herself. A twist of pink-and-white candy cane, that's what she is. Sweet enough to lick! She twirls right and left, admiring the way the fabric moves, the way it dances up her legs as she swings her body around. 'It is pretty this nightie, isn't it, Isabella?' says Sasha. 'I think it's my favourite one.'

At the end of the shrine is a ladder. Brendan and the girls climb up on to the roof. Blankets and cushions are laid out alongside pots of flowers – snowdrops, Christmas roses, cyclamen. While the girls wrap themselves in the blankets, Brendan lights incense and candles. The grey thread of smoke coils upwards to be snatched away by the breeze. The sea tugs back and forth. A group of birds fly in a V-shape across the bay.

When it starts to rain, they have to work quickly to roll up the blankets and gather up the candles and incense before everything becomes completely soaked. Inside the shrine, the girls lay everything out, trying to match how Brendan had arranged it all on the roof. Then, they lie side-by-side in silence. No windows, so all they have are the repetitive sounds of the outside world, while the shrine forms a protective shell around them. They listen to the rain tiptoeing across the roof, the endless drone of the sea. The girls feel comforted, calm. They like this place. Isabella softens towards Brendan. He was right – she won't tell him that – this simple space is correct. The only decorations within it are the dribbles of white paint that seeped inwards through the gaps in the planks of wood as they painted. She follows one of these drips from the start of its journey at the ceiling all the way down to the floor, where it has dried into a small, shiny egg shape.

'I don't remember anything from that day,' says Isabella.

'I remember the police car,' says Sasha. 'I remember Grandpa pacing the room. I remember Grandma phoning Uncle David, and I remember her crying.'

'I remember feeling dizzy, and thinking I couldn't breathe,' says Isabella. 'I couldn't sleep. Grandma came into the bedroom, then it's a blur.'

'What about friends?' asks Brendan. 'Do you have friends to talk to?'

'There aren't that many people on the island,' says Isabella.

'We have each other,' says Sasha.

'Mummy was lonely,' says Isabella.

'Some days, Mummy would barely speak. Daddy was easier to get along with. He didn't get annoyed if we were too scared to row across the bay on windy days. He'd let us off.'

'Mummy didn't like girls who were wimps,' says Isabella. 'She said girls should look after themselves, think for themselves, because that's what she said she had to do, and she said life won't treat a woman well, so she has to know how to treat herself well.'

When the rain clears, Brendan suggests a walk. The shoreline ahead is wet, a boggy mix of yellow grass, striated rocks, pebbly beaches that give way to a grass bank. They step over patches of seaweed, then around the rocks. On the other side of the jetty, the rowing boat is tied up to its mooring, rocking with the waves.

'Why don't we try it?' says Brendan.

They untie the ropes. The oars rest in the bottom of the boat. Brendan steps in first, holds his hand out to help the girls, but they ignore it, jumping straight past him. Once inside, Brendan takes the oars, Isabella the rudder. They turn in the opposite direction to the local village, heading east up the coastline, rounding the bay, working their way along the edge of the island. The water feels clean and alive. A glossy sheet of blue-black, broken only by wildlife: an otter comes up for air, a shoal of silver mackerel shatters the surface. They pass an empty house on the shore, the roof grown over with pale lichen, no glass left in any of the windows. The girls feel refreshed. They love being out here on the water, feeling the way they used to. Freedom, the gentle wind. No rules, no fear, no Anna and David telling them to be careful. Just like their kayaking trips with their mother. Even at six years old, they would bob on the water in small kayaks, following Rachel like little ducklings.

Brendan puts the oars down, lies back to let the water

carry them. The girls agree. Like this, they are knocked gently around by the waves. They float, drift away from the shore, then back in again, while gannets and kittiwakes circle overhead, playing in the air currents.

'What would happen if we didn't pick up the oars again?' asks Sasha.

'We'd wash up somewhere,' says Brendan. 'Everything washes up eventually.'

'But would we still be alive?' says Sasha.

'That would depend on how long it took you to wash up. And what kind of supplies you had in the boat. And whether or not you went mad after days out at sea.'

'Mad?' says Isabella.

'We're not going to go mad,' says Brendan. 'Here, girls, feel these.' Brendan flexes his arms. 'Like rock.'

The girls poke his biceps with their fingers. 'Yes,' they agree.

'These'll get you home.' He grins at them, then laughs. His blue eyes glitter when he laughs, the same way the glossy blue sea twinkles when the light hits it. Brendan lights a cigarette, lies out on the bench with arms crossed behind his head, feet dangling over the edge of the boat. On shore, the jagged cliffs guard a blanket of soft grass above them.

When they drift too far, Brendan picks up the oars, steers them back on course, lies back once more to finish his cigarette. The current carries them around into the second bay, but here, the benign wrinkles grow into deeper contours. The boat gently navigates them. The wind strengthens, sending spray over them. 'Hold on,' says Brendan, appearing scared. The water splits into deep dips and ridges, until eventually they feel as if they are surrounded by walls of sea. Brendan pulls out the life jackets from underneath the benches. The girls obediently put them on. They all hold on as the boat is thrown around, yet the girls aren't afraid. They've experienced this before, these sudden changes in the sea. They feel exhilaration at the boat's extraordinary journey up and down these cliffs of water, rising and plunging. The girls are wet, their hair soaked, their sight is blocked by water streaming down their red, cold faces, yet they yelp and whoop as they are thrown around. They enjoy Brendan's forced humility: he has to put down his oars. They are no use to him in this. Nor are his muscles. Only the girls know the secret: this will pass. Brendan holds on to either side of the boat – holds on for dear life – as they tunnel through the waves that threaten to topple them. Then, without warning, a sharp thud, a sudden jolt, like whiplash. They look around. They have washed up on the beach. The tide was on their side. Fields, hills, a couple of abandoned houses used as sheep pens. Disorientated, they step out of the boat. From the beach, the sea doesn't look as rough: just benign waves rolling in towards the shore.

'Come on, girls, let's get this further in, away from the water,' says Brendan.

Together, they drag the boat up the beach then sit to catch their breath.

'You were scared,' says Isabella.

'No I wasn't,' he snaps back.

But even still, he doesn't want to take the boat back. He tells the girls he's tired, they'll collect it another day. He tries to call David for a ride home but his phone won't switch on. Instead, they walk up the beach and inland along a track, heading past grazing sheep towards a tarmac road. They retrace their route on foot. It's a long walk, but the girls don't complain. Cold, wet, hungry, wrapped in the blankets they brought with them from the shrine, they trudge along. There's no rain, no cloud, just a bright cerulean sky, the sea a beautiful pale blue. The water gently crinkles into thin ribbons of white foam that ride up the shore, leaving behind delicate bubbles on the sand.

'Don't tell Anna and David about this experience. I might get into trouble for putting you in danger. They might try and stop us going out on the water again. And no one wants that.'

'Sure,' says Isabella.

'We won't say a thing,' says Sasha.

When they arrive back at the shrine, David and Anna are there. They've built a large circle with rocks, a fire lit within it. Anna has made tea. David has set up pieces of tree trunk as seats. The girls sit. Anna asks where they've been. 'Just a walk,' Isabella says airily.

'You're very wet,' replies Anna.

The girls shrug, feel relief when Anna doesn't pursue it. By evening, they're still out there, teeth chattering, but no one wants to go inside because the evening is so still. A faint orange glow from the fire, a thin trail of smoke snaking through the air, red and orange sparks. This is their shrine, and they want to stay here, listening to the sea.

That night, all is quiet. David and Anna have gone to bed, yet Brendan still has a light on, even though it's midnight. The girls whisper. He said they could go in any time they liked, not just if they felt scared or worried. 'All you have to do is knock,' were his words. They hesitate.

'But he said we could,' whispers Sasha.

The two of them shuffle at the door, whispering. Sasha turns to leave, but Isabella grabs her. 'Don't be a chicken!' she says.

They are about to knock, but stop themselves. It's late. What if he does mind? They begin shuffling about, giggling and hesitating, until they realise they're making so much noise he's probably heard them anyway and they have to go in, so they burst through the door without knocking. Brendan looks startled. He's sitting up in bed: white vest, chest hair poking out over the top of it, bare arms, faint sagging of the skin around his neck. He reminds Sasha of a cockerel. A tray in his lap, he is rolling cigarettes while sucking on a sweet. Beside him is an ashtray, which he looks at guiltily because it contains the wrinkled remains of at least twenty cigarettes, and he knows that Anna doesn't want him to smoke inside, because Rachel never allowed it.

'We're bored,' Sasha says.

'Well, what am I to do with two bored girls?' says Brendan.

'We knew you were smoking in here because we could smell it,' says Sasha.

'It's fine. I open the window.'

'So is this what you do? Sit in bed, rolling cigarettes?'

'While eating sweets,' says Brendan, holding up the bag of sherbet lemons by his bed. 'That's my evening task. Eating sweets and smoking.'

'At the same time?'

'That's disgusting,' says Isabella.

'No, it's delicious,' says Brendan.

The room is hot. Too hot. It feels muggy. There's a deep ledge on the tiny stone window to the left of his bed that Brendan clambers up on to. The glass is marbled with dirt and cobwebs. He opens it just a crack to send his smoke out through it, letting in a stream of ice-cold air as he does so.

'You don't mind?' he says, waving a cigarette at them. He beckons the girls towards him. 'Here,' he says, holding the cigarette out to them. 'Have you tried smoking before?'

The girls shake their heads.

'Try it,' he says.

Sasha goes first. Brendan holds it for her as she closes her lips around the end of it. A roll-up, without a proper tip, it feels cool and wet where Brendan has been puffing it. The wetness repulses her – even worse because it's cold – but she doesn't want to reveal this, so she sucks the smoke in. It takes concentration. She must breathe it in fully without coughing. It feels hard against her throat, jags against it, like a knife or a stone, and she can't contain herself any more. The smoke splutters out of her. It feels as if it's cutting her windpipe on its way back up. She keeps coughing. Brendan pats her back. She feels dizzy – hot and cold at the same time – and finds herself lying on his bed to recover. But Brendan ignores her, turning instead to Isabella – 'Your turn,' he says – which makes Sasha cross. She feels dreadful. Why is he paying her no attention? If nothing else, he could at least ask her if she's all right.

Isabella takes a puff, breathes it in, concentrating hard as she does so, because she also doesn't want to cough. She'd like to appear experienced. She leans up on to the window ledge, exhales the smoke in a perfect cylinder into the icy night. 'I like it,' says Isabella, going back in for a second puff. Brendan lets her, but when she goes for a third, he whips the cigarette away. 'You'll get addicted,' he says. 'Have a sweet instead.'

He holds out the bag. The girls' hands burrow inside it. 'Just one!' says Brendan, pulling Sasha's hand out of the bag. 'It's a pain getting to that shop, so I ration myself.'

But the girls don't give up. They catch each other's eyes. They want to tease Brendan, to cause mischief. They refuse to remove their hands from the bag, so in the end Brendan has no choice but to yank it away quite firmly.

'You two are jailbait.' He grins, holding the sweets above his head. Encouraged by his playfulness, Sasha jumps on to the bed, trying to bounce up high enough to grab them from him, but Brendan moves away, and so she lands with a thump on the ground. He goes to help her and, just as he is distracted, Isabella gets hold of the bag, running away with it, chased by Sasha.

'Shh,' whispers Brendan behind them. 'You'll wake Anna and David.'

In their room, they hide in the wardrobe, arms around each other.

'I'm going to find you,' Brendan says, creeping around the room. The girls hold on to the sweets, scared, as he searches for them, pulling back the bed covers, swishing open the curtains.

Without warning, Sasha jumps out of the wardrobe. 'You want them, don't you?' she says. She puts a sweet into her mouth with exaggerated slowness, sucks it noisily. 'Are you feeling cross?' she asks, waving the bag at him. Sasha hands her sister a sweet – she does it slowly, smiling archly at Brendan. She enjoys the look of confusion on his face, his powerlessness, because he isn't allowed to manhandle them, and she knows it.

'Hmm,' Isabella says to Brendan. 'This is delicious. I bet you want your sweets back.' She waves the bag in front of his face, then snaps her hand behind her back before he can grab it.

Brendan is smiling now. 'You girls,' he says. 'You naughty girls.'

'You're not having one,' Isabella says. 'We're going to eat them all.' They take another sweet each, two sweets at a time in their mouths. No longer able to speak, cheeks bulging, they try not to laugh.

'Actually, I don't want them anyway,' Brendan says. Abruptly, he stands up, surprising the girls. He heads towards the door, but stops before leaving to turn back and say: 'It's not good for girls to be eating all those sweets. You'll get fat.' He closes the door behind him.

The girls are left alone, their mouths crammed. They feel sick. As soon as they are sure that Brendan is gone, they start laughing, spitting the sweets out into their hands – they didn't want them anyway – but they've got his bag of sweets, which makes them laugh even more. And they're not going to give them back.

Brendan asks David if he'll help him retrieve the abandoned rowing boat. Sasha and Isabella remain obediently silent while he lies, telling David he went off in it alone, got into trouble when the weather changed so left it behind to walk back. 'It was the safest thing to do,' Brendan says.

David agrees to help, so the four of them – Brendan, David, the two girls – walk along the empty tarmac road. The air is icy and fresh. It feels like eucalyptus on their skin. The boat is closer than the girls remember. In no time, they arrive at the field of grazing sheep, slip along the track and arrive at the shore, where they find the boat still nestled in between sand and grass, at exactly the point they left it. They flip it over. Brendan and David drag it over the sand and down to the water.

David takes a seat on the forward thwart and picks up the oars, while Brendan helps Sasha and Isabella into their seat. A tussle ensues. No space for Brendan. The boat is small. He can't comfortably squeeze in beside David. They'll be too squashed. The only possibility would be to sit on the floor of the boat, but it will be damp, and they have no idea how long it will take to get back.

'You walk,' says David. 'We'll meet you back at the house.'

Brendan draws breath as if he's going to argue back, but then stops himself. 'Fine,' he says crossly, turning on his heels. He trudges through the soft sand, back up towards the road.

Using an oar, David pushes the boat into deeper water. Against the tide, progress is slow. They spot Brendan sulkily marching back up the coast road towards the house. The further out to sea they get, the harder David must row to keep them moving. To keep the girls happy, he starts a game: name the birds flying overhead. Sasha is the quickest. She knows them all: the gannets, sea eagles, auks, guillemots, razorbills, kittiwakes. She has a scrapbook in which she collects the names and pictures of all these birds. Anna and David gave it for her birthday one year, along with a set of crayons. She'd spent hours in the library outlining the birds in pencil, colouring them in, and because of this, she wouldn't go out shooting with Peter, so he used to take Isabella instead. They came home with pheasants or grouse, sometimes a wood pigeon. Sasha hated it. It made her cry.

Even worse, Isabella would help pluck them, dropping bloodied feathers on to sheets of newspaper in the kitchen. Sasha would take the feathers out to the garden to bury them in little square graves she dug with a soup spoon. She hated this side of her father – this barbaric, violent side that killed beautiful animals. Sometimes, she preferred to be with David, because he was gentle. She couldn't imagine him doing anything as cruel as hurting an animal.

Brendan is already at the shrine when, finally, David ties the boat on to the small jetty. Sasha returns to the house with David so she can fetch her sketching things, while Isabella stays at the shrine with Brendan.

Inside the shrine, Isabella peeks through a crack at the sea.

Brendan pulls out a cigarette and lights it. 'You don't mind, do you?' he says to Isabella.

She shakes her head. He puffs at it, then holds the cigarette up, waving it in her direction. He shifts along the edge of the mattress to make space for her. She awkwardly purses her lips around the cigarette – she's still learning, even if she doesn't want him to know that – sucking at it until the end of the cigarette glows. She draws the smoke down into her lungs. They pass the cigarette back and forth. She grows in confidence with each puff. The smoke feels less like something rasping at her throat, becomes more familiar, smoother, each time she has a go.

'I was very hurt you all left me out of the boat,' says Brendan.

151

'We didn't mean to,' says Isabella.

'I didn't like it,' says Brendan.

'We're both very happy that you're here. I'm sorry. I think we'd have been very bored if you hadn't come to stay,' says Isabella. Brendan hands her back the cigarette, which she takes. 'I find Anna and David a bit boring,' she says.

With only the blank walls and the sound of the sea, Isabella feels protected. She can't see outside, so the wilderness beyond is just a feeling, a series of sounds, as if it's not a real place but an imaginary one inside her head. She closes her eyes to intensify the sounds, smokes some more. A dreamy, spreading blur dissolves across her body, through her head, her chest, along her arms. When she gives Brendan the cigarette back, something takes over that she can't explain: she grabs his hand, clings to it. He doesn't seem to mind. Instead, his warm, solid fingers settle into the tight spaces between her own slim fingers. While she carries on smoking, he strokes her hand. It feels transgressive, exciting, as if he's communicating a wordless message. The rhythmic warmth of his hand is soothing, sedating; it's a drug that is carrying her off to a place where longing surfaces within her. But the longing isn't pleasant or dreamy; it's like a sharp pain, a void in the cavity of her chest, as if the air has been sucked out of her. An un-fillable space. She doesn't want to let go of his warm, comforting hand. She feels dizzy from the smoke. She needs to lie down. Can she lay her head on his stomach?

'Yes,' he whispers.

She lies on him, her head rising and falling in time to the rhythm of his breath. He gently strokes her hair. His tenderness soothes the pain of her longing. She feels herself helplessly tumbling towards his soft promise, falling and falling further into intense wordlessness. She's unwilling to stop, unable to stop, and she misses her father so fiercely that the only thing preventing her from completely disintegrating is the touch of Brendan's hand against her head.

That night, the girls awake to find Brendan in their bedroom, standing over them, urging them to get up.

'Get dressed. I have something for you,' he says.

The girls struggle to understand what is happening. It's the middle of the night. He's holding a torch. They screw up their faces, grimacing against the light.

'I promise you,' he says. 'It'll be worth it.'

They rub their eyes, get out of bed. Brendan waits outside the bedroom while they get dressed.

'Dress up warm,' he whispers through the door.

Downstairs, the three of them go out into the night. The full moon casts shadows as strongly as if it was the midday sun. The moon shimmers on the surface of the sea. At the shrine, Brendan has already lit a fire. The wood is stacked high, so the flames leap into the air. The girls stand by it, warming their hands. A flame jumps too high, scurries up a tree like a squirrel. They shout out to Brendan to come – it's going to set the tree alight, there'll be a forest fire – but

Brendan doesn't react. The tree is damp. The spark smokes, then dies, and once again the girls feel safe.

Brendan opens the door to the shrine. 'I've been hard at work,' he says.

Inside, it's alight with small, flickering candles set in glass jars.

Hammered into the wall is a blanket, dividing the space in half. Brendan asks the girls to sit on one side of it, while he will take the place opposite them. But before they begin, he needs to explain the rules of the game. While he's talking, Isabella inspects him. Her eyes flicker over the softness of his jaw line, the way the skin folds as he looks downward. Around his mouth, the beginnings of looseness. He is old. And yet he hasn't gone grey or lost his hair. The sweater he wears contours his shoulders, so that Isabella can see that they are strong and square, not sloping. He looks at her to find her watching him. Their eyes meet briefly. He doesn't look away. Blue eyes, rimmed with dark lashes.

'I need to explain the rules,' Brendan says. 'It's called the confession game. You say "Forgive me father, for I have sinned," and you tell me all the naughty things you've done – for example, helping yourself to my sweets – and then I tell you what your punishment is going to be.'

'What if we haven't done any naughty things?' says Sasha.

'Well, I know for a fact that you have,' says Brendan. 'Time to begin.'

He disappears around the other side of the blanket. The girls sit cross-legged opposite each other. They're enjoying it. Brendan's mad, but he's fun. They squirm in their seats – what will the punishment be? Will there be prizes too? They fidget, nervous, sitting up straight, wondering who is going to go first.

'How long is it since your last confession?' begins Brendan.

The girls snicker. They hide their mouths behind their hands, they can't quite gauge Brendan. He's solemn. Is this actually a game, as he said it was? His voice is serious, his tone deep. Is he going to try to make them say things? They ought to say things, they ought to do as they're told.

'Forever,' says Isabella.

'We've never done confession, because we're not Catholics,' says Sasha.

'We're not even Christians. We're not christened, and we never went to church,' says Isabella.

Brendan's head appears around the curtain. 'So what you do, you say, "Forgive me father, for I have sinned," then you tell me what you've done.' The curtain drops. The girls hear Brendan shuffling back into position.

'Forgive me father for I have sinned, for I stole Brendan's sweets,' says Isabella.

'And when did you take the sweets?' asks Brendan.

'Last night, Brendan. You know that,' says Sasha.

'Last night?' he repeats.

155

'Yes, last night,' Isabella snaps.

'Last night. You've never before taken sweets from my room?'

The girls hesitate. Their eyes meet. They fall silent. Sasha feels heat travelling through her stomach.

'Just last night.'

'So never before last night have you been into my room?'

'No,' says Isabella emphatically.

'So was it the tooth fairy who left footprints all over my bed?'

The girls say nothing.

'I know for a fact that you told Anna that I went into your room, and that you told her that I'd upset you, so why would you go into *my* room without asking?'

Silence.

'And I'd like to know what it was that you looked at, and what it was that you took?'

'We took two sweets,' says Isabella emphatically.

'That's all?'

'Two sweets. Nothing else. We didn't think you'd mind,' says Sasha.

'But how come you thought I wouldn't mind you doing that, when you went telling tales to Anna about me?'

'It was a mistake,' says Isabella. She gets up, heads towards the exit, but Brendan quickly pulls back the curtain, rushes to the door and stands in front of it.

'You can't go. No,' he says. 'I came up here to help you, and you complained about me, and I got told off by Anna, and then you did exactly the same thing to me. What am I supposed to think?'

'We didn't mean any harm,' says Sasha. She can feel the tears begin to well up inside her. The door is barred. She's trapped, scared. She wants to go home. 'We like you, Brendan. We appreciate everything you're doing for us. We just thought you wouldn't mind. We can buy you some more sweets. We have money in our room.'

They're scared, they want to go home. A thin wail out in the darkness beyond the shrine chills the girls, sets them grabbing for one another.

'I don't want to play this game any more,' Sasha says.

Then, Brendan's face cracks. He grins, starts to laugh. His arms widening towards both of them, pulling them in for an embrace. 'I'm just joking with you both. I don't care that you went into my room. I have nothing to hide. Did you find anything interesting?'

'Nothing. Your washbag. The sweets,' says Sasha. 'Nothing more. We didn't look. We promise.'

Brendan lights up a cigarette. 'It just brings me to an important point. Trust. Lies. Honesty. All good relationships are built on trust and honesty. We've got to have trust between us if I'm going to help you.'

'Yes, yes, you can trust us,' says Sasha. 'We promise. We only said to Anna that you came into our room because we wanted to see what she'd do.'

'They brought you to our house without asking us. This is our home, and they didn't ask us if it was OK, they just brought you here, like it was *their* home, so we decided to cause some problems, to remind them they can't just do whatever they want,' says Isabella.

'And we're sorry.' Sasha's eyes are wide open. A tear slides down her cheek.

'Please don't be scared of me again. I'm not scary. You have nothing to fear with me. I'm here to look after you, to help you,' says Brendan. 'I just wanted to set some boundaries between us.'

'So we can forget about it?' says Isabella.

In the corner of the room is a small, canvas rucksack, from which Brendan produces some typed sheets of paper. He asks both girls to lie down on the mattress and close their eyes. They shuffle into place, arms by their sides. They must keep their eyes shut. They feel him laying blankets across them. The temptation is too much, and Isabella peeks.

'Close!' whispers Brendan.

Isabella feels something soft around her eyes. He lifts her head, ties something at the back, rests her head back down. A blindfold?

'I'll take it off when it's over,' he says.

He does the same to Sasha. Then, a rustling of papers, liquid swilling. Is he taking a swig of something? Is it for them? Isabella opens her eyes under the blindfold, but all she can see is a slit of light. She daren't move her head to see what Brendan is doing. She hears shuffling close by. Perhaps he's sitting next to them.

'Deep breath in.'

The girls inhale.

'Deep breath out.'

They exhale.

'I'm going to hypnotise you,' he says. 'Regress you. Take you back to the time you were children.'

'Why?' asks Isabella.

'You'll see,' says Brendan.

He tells the girls to relax, to breathe deeply. He counts back from ten to one, tells them to go deeper into trance. Incense. Sandalwood? Amber? He keeps counting. The girls feel themselves relax and soften, their muscles melting into the mattress. The smell. The darkness. The soft, cool feel of the blindfolds against their skin. *Go deeper into trance.* Brendan repeats the words. Isabella feels her mouth fall open. She doesn't bother to close it, too relaxed, no energy. Brendan asks them to imagine a beautiful lake, surrounded by forests. They must imagine swimming underwater – it's completely safe, no hazards – and they can breathe. Both girls imagine the same blue water, soft white sand beneath, exploring it all, while all the time, Brendan is urging them to go deeper, deeper, further down, relax, let themselves fall.

When they are under hypnosis, he wants them to regress, to imagine a time when they were little, but Isabella arrives at a wall she can't move beyond. She wants Brendan to stop, and she says so, but he tells her 'Have no fear,' and keeps pushing. They must go back as far as they can. He wants to take them to ten years old, seven, five, three – then a memory comes to Isabella. She's in the garden, holding a snail, trying to get it to stick to a leaf but it won't stick, and keeps falling. Isabella feels a hand on her chest. Brendan is in the middle of the two mattresses. He asks the girls to begin panting. If they force the out-breath, the in-breath will happen instinctively. The girls hesitate.

'Come on,' he says. 'I'll show you.' Brendan forces his breath out – the sound is like ripping paper, it lands on their cheeks. Tobacco. Horrible.

But the girls feel they have no choice but to do the same. They force a breath out and then their lungs automatically fill the empty space. The in-breath is like a reflex, and they begin to pant. Brendan holds them down with his hands. They continue to pant. They lose track of time. Isabella gets pins and needles. First in her hands, her legs, then across her whole body. Her head feels hot. It burns. She shakes. She can no longer feel her fingers or toes; her arms are stiff and heavy by her side. She's numb, but Brendan says she must carry on with the breathing. They want to stop – it's making them dizzy – but he says they mustn't. It's the process: they must pant.

'And this is the final stage,' he says.

Isabella feels a blanket held around her, over her head, over her whole body. Brendan is on top of her, his arms either side. He holds the blanket down over her, trapping her. It's hot, itchy on her face. She can't move. Brendan is urging her to keep panting, but she can't. She's hot, she's trapped, this blanket won't let her move, but still, instinctively, she pushes against it, trying to free herself. Brendan is fighting back. If she moves to the left, he moves too. 'You must fight your way out,' he says. She struggles. He's strong. The blanket forms a wall against her, it gives only a little when she pushes against it. She keeps trying to free herself, until eventually she screams out, 'I can't breathe. Let me go.'

Sasha sits up, removes her blindfold. 'Let her go, Brendan. What are you doing?'

He calls for calm. It's fine. It's part of the process. 'This is how you're reborn,' he says. 'You struggle your way out into the world, just as you did fifteen years ago.'

He holds Sasha back with one arm, while continuing to use his other arm, as well as both of his legs, to ensure that Isabella remains trapped underneath the blanket.

'Let me out,' she yells.

Brendan is steadfast. 'Sometimes, in order to find the light, we do need to go deep into the darkness,' he says.

Sasha is in tears now. It's dark. She's frightened. The candles flicker in the breeze as Isabella and Brendan struggle. Then, suddenly, Brendan is thrown back against the floor with the blanket over him and Isabella – sweating, breathless – is sitting up. She bursts into tears.

'It's over,' says Brendan. 'You did it.' She collapses into his arms, and he holds her, strokes her hair, comforts her, while she clings to him with all the vulnerability of a newborn. 'You made it out. How do you feel?'

161

Sasha is confused, angry. 'Brendan, you can't do this to us,' she snaps.

Isabella is sodden with sweat, still limp in Brendan's arms. 'No, Sasha,' she says. 'It was amazing. You should try it. I saw lights. I felt things, like a freeing, a liberation. It was amazing.' She breaks away from Brendan, her cheeks still wet with tears. 'Amazing,' she says again, breathlessly.

Outside, Brendan beckons the girls to sit. He rolls a skin drum towards them. 'I brought this for us to make some music. Let's enjoy ourselves,' he says. He shows them more instruments he has with him. Thick tubes of bamboo to blow through or bang with sticks. 'Be creative,' he says, handing them to the girls. 'Do what you feel like doing. Follow your instincts.'

Brendan goes first with the drum, making low, slow thudding. Isabella picks up a stick, starts banging it against the bamboo tube. Together, they manage to create an approximation of music, which makes Sasha start dancing. As Brendan beats, she jumps in the air, pounding the earth with her feet, keeping time, breaking into laughter as she picks up a log, throws it on to the fire. The flames leap up, sparks crackle in the air, the drum hangs at waist height from Brendan's neck. His arms in the air, embracing the heavens, then swooping down to bang the drum in a frenzy of movement and rhythm. The girls are drunk with it now, dancing around the fire, jumping around it, faces lit redly from beneath, weaving in and out of it and each other, banging the drum, the sticks, the bamboo tubes, giddy with happiness, whooping and jumping, spinning around the fire, their laughter turning hysterical as they jump and bound, united in love and sorrow and the deep, rhythmic sound of the drum's beat.

All night they dance, until they're exhausted. Inside the shrine, Sasha flops on to a mattress, immediately drifts off to sleep, but Isabella doesn't. She can't. She's still full of energy, on a high, so she sits beside Brendan, who is rolling a cigarette. The soft flutter of Sasha's breath beside them makes their secret seem all the more alive. They are here again, together, alone. He lights up a cigarette, puffs, hands it to her. She has to suppress a coughing fit, but she likes how grown up smoking makes her feel. She likes sitting close to Brendan, feeling the warmth of his arm. His body against hers is reassuring – as if he might belong to her. Then his arm wriggles around behind her, his hand on her shoulder. He feels it too. It holds her firmly, holds her together. He must like her, too, in this way, because otherwise he wouldn't be here, wouldn't have his arm around her. This closeness feels like a privilege, a dangerous excitement that flutters between them. He strokes her shoulder. This glittering feeling arises within her, as if something vaporous and mutable has been changed into something solid and touchable. Again, this warmth, this soft promise, this tumbling. She nudges him. Would he like the cigarette? He takes it. It feels as if they're making a pact. But who will enter whose world? If he enters hers, they'll both be teenagers, nervously pushing together towards a new experience (he only pretending), so perhaps he will bring her into his world, where she'll be alone with him, as an adult, hiding the danger that she feels as he propels her carelessly towards a new experience. Will he know she'll be terrified? Will he care?

But she wants to feel the surety of being an adult, where meaning is fixed, and everyone understands the world and their place within it. She wants this certainty, craves it. She won't feel terrified, she knows she won't, because she is adventurous, as her mother was, so she leans up with a disturbing excitement all over her. As she turns her head awkwardly towards his, her lips searching to drink in more of his warmth, of his reassurance, they land on his lips, which remain still and cold. So she tries harder, but still they are unmoving, even as she presses more and more, the force of them trying to prise open his mouth, demanding that he give her the thing that he promised her. A hand on each of her shoulders pushes her away. She feels hot with confusion and humiliation. Why the suddenness of his withdrawal? He looks startled – as if someone has thrown cold water over him. Isabella is hurt, even more so because she knows he, too, was lost in this hypnotic moment: he played with it, played with her, danced at the edge of this forbidden pleasure, because he believed himself to be in control.

'No, Isabella. No,' he says. 'You've mis . . .'

She feels shame, fury. For a moment, they are both silent. He tries to take her hand, but she snatches it away from him.

'I want you to leave me alone,' she says.

'I understand,' he replies.

She hands him back his cigarette, his nasty, stinking cigarette, that makes her feel as if all that is bitter and harmful and disgusting in the world has been contained in one clenched fist and crammed inside her mouth. He takes it, and leaves.

Through a crack in the shrine wall, she watches him walk up towards the house. The tip of the cigarette glows red each time he takes a puff, nonchalantly smoking, without a care in the world. Because of that, Isabella hates him even harder. She's too angry to cry. She shuffles under the blanket beside her sister. There is barely enough room, but she doesn't care because she is safe. This is where she belongs. She puts her arm over her sister's body, drawing her in towards her. Sasha stirs, but doesn't wake. The sea relentlessly laps the shore. An owl torments the dark. Isabella pulls the covers over her, all of her, including her head, so that she is hidden. Her cheeks feel hot, sweating, her throat constricts. She feels too solid. She wants to evaporate, to dissolve into nothing but her body is stubbornly insistent. It is the conduit for this surge of heat and flow and effervescence that feels like agony and won't go away.

When the girls awake, their bones are stiff from the cold. Outside, the cinders of the fire are still smoking. The night before is a confusing blur. There's so much they can't remember. 'When did we fall asleep?' asks Sasha.

'I don't know,' says Isabella.

'Me neither.'

Outside, Isabella breaks into a run, wanting to get inside the house and up to bed before anyone else is up. She doesn't want to see Brendan or to hear him. She's a piece of glass that might shatter at the sound of his voice. It would have been easier if he'd just punched her in the eye. In her own room, under the covers, time slows, magnifying her memory of the previous evening, distorting it. Her skin burns. It comes back to her as a surge of heat that courses through her body, makes her want to run, to find a place to go and never be seen again. She pulls the duvet over herself and hides. Perhaps like this she can hide forever, and never see him again.

warm water

THE NEXT DAY IS GLORIOUS. THE SEA TWINKLES. THE GRASS
shines glossy and green. Puffy white clouds foam happily in
the sky. Brendan and David are loading the tractor with
firewood to take down to the shrine. They want to know
who's going with them. Isabella refuses. She's been sullen
all morning. She'll barely speak to any of the adults, won't
do anything anyone asks of her. She wants to go down to
the village, walk along the sea wall out towards the ruins.
She'd like Sasha to go with her, but Sasha says David told
her there's still much work to do at the shrine – stacking
firewood, clearing fallen branches, gathering more stones
to build up the wall around their fire pit – and he wants
them to help. Sasha doesn't want to upset them.

'Fuck them both,' Isabella whispers. 'I'm not going, and
I don't want you to go, either.'

So the men go alone to the shrine. The girls head off
across the hill towards the village. Anna runs a bath.

The huge old cast-iron tub is so deep she feels lost in it.

Her head barely rises above the edge. She lies there for an hour, skin wrinkling, turning the hot tap on with her toe when she needs more heat. Anna wouldn't usually lounge in the bath all morning. If her mother were still alive and with her up at the house, it wouldn't be allowed, even at her age. They'd be out in the garden, finding winter blooms – catkins, a willow branch – for the table, or organising lunch. They'd be constantly thinking about all the things that needed to be done, and only then would they go for a walk or browse through the library or have a glass of sherry together in the evening. If her mother was there, they'd have a quaint reciprocal existence: you wash, I'll dry. Anna would go along with this, because she was well-trained not to resist. She wasn't used to questioning whether the things she was doing were actually the things she wanted to do. She did as she was told, out of habit. Her mother was the same: able to live within the unconscious restraint of what was required, of what others might think. Anna still misses her. Avery – and not just Avery, other friends too – told her that, alongside the many emotions they felt at their parents' deaths, there was also a feeling of freedom at being released from the role of child. But Anna doesn't feel like that. She still misses the feeling of reassurance that the world her mother presented to her was the world that actually existed: everything made sense when it was seen through her mother's eyes. For many years, Anna kept her blue handbag hanging in her wardrobe. As a child, she'd found it full of mystery: lipsticks, powder compacts, tiny vials of perfume, and a red purse that zipped up so tightly Anna could never get it undone to peek inside. Her mother used to keep the bag on a peg in the kitchen. It marked whether she was in or out, whether her world was constant and knowable, or uncertain and unanchored. After her mother's death, Anna kept the bag. It still had the power to reassure, to communicate a stable world to her, give a constancy of meaning. It took a long time, and encouragement from David, before she felt able to take it down to the charity shop. She handed it over, wrapped in pink tissue paper – it felt as if she was giving away her own baby – then turned to leave the shop with the feeling of not being in her own body. Her physical-self had been compelled to do something her emotional-self couldn't comprehend. *It's only a handbag*, she repeated in her head as she went down the street. At home, she sobbed again, just as she had at her mother's funeral, when she'd sobbed loudly, messily, at the thought of her mother's wasted life, of all that she might have been, had she not chosen to live within the shadow of her husband. Anna had spent much of the wake locked in the bathroom, trying to pull herself together. Yet no matter how sternly she told herself she must go downstairs to be with the guests – it's what her mother would have wanted, expected, her to do – she couldn't do it. She sat in an empty bath, wearing her black clothes, playing with a shell-shaped cake of soap. The only person she wanted to see was Avery, who came and lay in the bath with her, topping and tailing, with all their clothes on.

Later, when everyone had gone, Anna went for a walk through the fields that surrounded her childhood home. She walked past pretty fields of wheat backlit by the sun, and realised her mother had never expressed any kind of rage. It didn't even sneak out. She never made snide comments, never sulked, never sabotaged. Perhaps her mother didn't see herself as wasting her life, because if she did, the anger would have found its way out. Why had Anna insisted on cloaking her in failure? Perhaps her mother really did hate being the centre of attention, really didn't need accolades and validation. She played her piano as she wanted, in private. Her evenings spent upstairs when Anna's father's friends came over were not terrified retreats but moments of quiet liberation. Anna wondered if her mother's life was one of finding joy privately, in simplicity. Not caring what anyone else thinks: isn't this what they call success?

Anna had tried to rebel from her mother's life. She made choices for herself, she went to art school to study graphic design, and even though she felt so small and conservative around all these men in their denim jackets, with their roll-ups and radical political views, she stuck with it. She spent hours cutting out little pieces of tracing paper to cover the letters on a sheet, making book covers, letterheads, re-imaginings of the Tube logo. She graduated and got a job with a small design studio. She had a proper job! Not like her mother at all.

When the water begins to cool, Anna turns the tap, but only a trickle comes out. She turns it further, as far as it will go. Still nothing. So she gets out of the bath, wraps herself in a towel and heads to her room, but is halted by the sight of brown, rusty water streaming down the landing wall, making a pool on the floor. She runs downstairs, fetches a couple of plastic buckets, wedges them in close to the wall, but two isn't enough, so she runs back for more. Another leak springs, this time in the downstairs hall, where it's threatening to damage paintings and a silk sofa. She removes her towel – the only thing she has – to pad into a corner to catch the water while she runs naked into the kitchen to find pans, bowls, anything she can use. Above her, water bubbles through the ceiling. Anna drags the furniture away from it, takes paintings down, ferries them to the kitchen where it's dry. She gathers more towels, dries walls wherever she can, mops up water from the carpets, rolls tea towels around the buckets, all the time naked, the flow from the ceilings refuses to stop. Then: Jerri's list of instructions! Anna pulls it out of the drawer in the kitchen. She sweeps everything out from beneath the sink, on to the floor, pulls the mains lever at the back. Upstairs, the flow of water slows, peters out to a trickle, eventually stops altogether.

Anna dresses, fetches David and Brendan from the shrine. Brendan goes to check the attic, but returns to say that he cannot find the source of the problem, and that the attic is a mess: pools of water, damp walls, swollen floor-boards.

David calls a local plumber with no success. There is

only one who regularly serves the islands, and he can't come for three days.

'We can find a way,' says Brendan.

In the garage, he finds a blue plastic drum, takes it down to the sea on the back of the tractor. At the shore, he goes back and forth with a bucket, filling the drum with seawater. He then ferries the drum back, manoeuvres it into the house, then into the downstairs toilet, where he puts a plastic jug on the shelf next to it.

'The toilet can flush with this,' he says.

Another drum, filled this time with water from the pond rather than the sea, will stand in the kitchen for them to rinse the dishes. For cooking and drinking, David goes to the nearest shop to buy bottled water.

'Let's just go back to London,' Anna says when he gets back.

'The plumber will come,' replies Brendan.

'And washing ourselves?'

'It's only three days, Anna,' says Brendan.

'Perhaps a local leisure centre,' says David. 'At the swimming pool.'

'A leisure centre?' asks Anna. 'Where?'

'There must be one. Even if it's a few boat rides away,' says David.

'We're not ready to go back to London,' says Brendan. 'There's still work to be done. With the girls.'

'And heating? We can't run the central heating if there's no water in the system,' says Anna.

172

'The fires. Warm sweaters,' replies Brendan.

In the end, David finds a supply of oil radiators up in the attic. He dusts them off with a cloth, rigs them up throughout the house. With the dials turned up to high, they provide a little warmth, but even so, when night comes, Anna climbs into bed to sleep in all her clothes.

* * *

It's five in the evening, the next day. Brendan said he would refill the drums of water but hasn't done it: not the drum in the kitchen for washing-up, or – more importantly – the one in the bathroom, where Anna finds herself standing, her trousers pulled down to her knees, wondering what she is going to do if she can't flush. She changes her mind, pulls up her trousers, takes the spade Brendan left by the door and heads out into the woods with a torch. She holds the spade with one hand, a toilet roll in the other, begins digging her hole. The earth is solid. She needs all her strength to break through its surface. Using all her weight on the spade, it eventually slides into the earth. She wrestles with it until the hole is big enough to crouch over. She pulls down her trousers, feels the pinch of the cold on her bare skin. She tries to balance, to keep her feet steady. Her shit lands with a soft thud in the hole. The steam that rises from it is illuminated by the beam of the torch. She cleans herself and tosses the paper into the hole, which immediately extinguishes the steam – as well as the disgust she feels at

173

herself. She pulls up her trousers, kicks soil into the hole, covering it. She stamps down so the earth is compacted. Back at the house, Anna leans the shovel by the back door, goes to wash her hands. No water. It's only been two days, and already she can smell herself.

'Have you seen the girls?' says David. Behind him stands Brendan. 'They said they were going for a walk, and we haven't seen them since. Did they come home?'

'No,' says Anna.

'Did they say anything to you?' asks David. 'It's getting dark, and they're nowhere to be found.'

Anna fetches torches from the basket by the door, hands them out, but David says he'll take the car. Anna walks through the trees, searching with the torch for footprints, for any sign of them. The headlights of the Land Rover zigzag through the fields, swinging to the right and left. Brendan goes off in a different direction. As Anna calls out for the girls, she hears her words echoed by Brendan, who is on the other side of the house, heading up the hill, bellowing out for the girls to please respond.

They've been out for hours, but still no sign. Anna's torch is trained to the ground as she picks her way along the path. She navigates around rocks, climbing them, jumping off, all the time shouting out. It's pointless. The adults will never win a game of hide-and-seek with the girls, not in this place; they'll be found when they feel like being found. Anna turns towards the shore where the rocks are smoother, the sand easier to walk on. It's cold. The girls will not be able to remain outside for much longer in this. The ends of Anna's fingers are numb. She puts one hand at a time in her pockets, using the other to hold the torch, but it makes it more difficult to balance. She steps up on to a rock to keep moving across the beach, but it's wet. She slips, then as she tries to regain her balance, the torch flies out of her hand. She tugs her other hand from her pocket, but it's stuck. She can't break her fall, so lands on her right ankle, which bends, causing a sharp pain. Her cheek hits the side of the rock. Wet sand beneath her, trousers absorbing the cold. She's dizzy. It's dark. Her ankle throbs. Should she call out for Brendan and David? They won't hear her, not above the sound of the sea. Instead, she manages to pull herself to her feet, but she can't walk. She goes back down on to all fours, crawls along the shore until she reaches the trees. She finds a stick strong enough to support her and, with it, she stands. She limps slowly back to the house.

'Anna, you're bleeding,' says Brendan.

Brendan helps her into a seat. David fetches ice, some tissues, which he uses to dab at Anna's face. 'What happened?'

'I don't think it's broken,' says Brendan, who has removed Anna's shoe and sock, and is examining her foot.

'There is some sand in the wound. We'll need water to clean it,' says David.

Brendan fetches a bottle from his car, tips it into a small bowl, hands David more tissues. David wets the tissue, squeezes water from it, then dabs. Anna feels the cool water pour down her cheek, along her jawline, into her neck. As he dabs and rinses, the water in the bowl turns from clear to pale pink.

'The wound is clean,' says David. 'It's only a small cut. A plaster will be enough.'

Anna takes a dry tissue from the table, dabs at her eyes. She is the child now, being tended to, unable to stop the tears. Then the door opens. The girls.

'Where have you been?' shouts David. 'We've been searching everywhere.'

Sasha's head is bowed, but Isabella is unmoved by David's anger. She glares back at him, haughty and accusing.

'Look at what you've done to Anna,' he snaps. 'And after everything we've done for you.'

Isabella snorts. She grabs her sister's arm, pulls her along too. They swish out of the room.

'Ungrateful little madam,' snaps David.

'It's not their fault,' says Anna.

'They can't treat us with such disrespect,' says David.

When the girls return an hour or so later, they're like two little girls again, far younger than their years as they hug hot water bottles. Isabella's is in the shape of an elephant, fluffy and grey, big fur ears lined with pink, and a short, stubby trunk. Sasha's is a rhino, with a stuffed horn and two plastic eyes. 'We're cold,' says Sasha.

With a sigh, David stands up. He empties the last of Brendan's bottle of water into the kettle, waits for it to boil, fills each animal. Holding them close to their chests, wearing their nighties, they head back upstairs, followed by David.

When, eventually, Anna is helped up the stairs by Brendan, David is already asleep. The shutters are open. The full moon beams down into the room, making elongated replicas of the windows on the floor. David is lit in thick pieces of silver-grey light. By his side, the duvet has fallen to the floor. Anna picks it up, tucks David in again. Immediately, he turns, treading the covers away so that, once again, they lie crumpled beside him. This time, she picks up the duvet to wrap around herself. She hobbles out to the balcony, where she runs her fingers along the stone balustrade. Beyond her, the sky stretches. She pulls the duvet closer around herself. A clear, crisp night. Stars joined together with wisps of light, the Milky Way threading across the sky. The London sky is bland in comparison, bleached by street lights. But up here, all these little stars puncture holes in the blackness. A wild landscape of its own. Savage. Another world. A mystery opening out before her. The endlessness is overwhelming. Below it, the shrine is lit by the moon. A silver-grey square shimmering in the dark.

'I hate that fucking shrine,' Anna mutters to herself. She doesn't understand why it evokes such a strong reaction in her. It's only four walls and a roof. A project for the girls.

Back inside, she gets into bed, rolls in close to David, sleeps. Later, she is awoken by the click of the door handle.

177

The door creaks open, a shaft of soft, reflected light, a shape appearing in that shaft of light. Through half-open eyes, she sees Sasha shake David awake.

'Isabella's upset,' Sasha whispers. 'She wants you.'

Automatically, David pulls back his covers, climbs out of the bed, follows the girl.

'Should I come too?' Anna whispers. David tells her to get some sleep. He'll manage.

Anna stares at the ceiling, following the map of cracks and shapes. Do girls find safe men, against whom they can test their power, find out what they are capable of? Do they need a trustworthy man like David to work out whether this 'I' that I am is powerful enough? If there is a moment a girl discovers her power, then is there a contrasting moment when a woman loses hers? Anna stops the thought. No point following that particular trail. It will lead to nowhere. I'm not fragile, Anna thinks. I'm not fragile like David is. I'm not falling apart. It is David who is falling apart. It is David who is being undone by these girls, by this thankless task, not me.

Anna leaves the house to walk up to the hill towards the cairn with her phone. A thick fog leaks across the landscape like poured milk. It hovers above the sea for miles out. She sticks to the narrow path that cuts upwards through the thick brown bracken. At the cairn, she sits, using its wide conical shape to protect her from the wind. As soon as she switches on her phone, it pings with a voicemail. Avery.

She's worried. Anna's cat is lonely. The neighbour, Jane, has been going in daily. Avery's been going in when she can, but still, the cat is not at all happy. She won't eat, won't go out, spends all day curled up on Anna's side of the bed, sleeping mournfully. 'I don't want to give you more things to worry about,' says Avery's message, 'but Jane and I think the cat is depressed.'

Anna has only left the cat for more than a month once before, when her mother was ill. Even though David was with her – she was never completely alone – the cat was furious when Anna returned. She swished off into the garden and sat under a tree, where she stared back into the house with intense, furious eyes. David could go off for as long as he liked – the cat couldn't have cared less – but when Anna abandoned her, the reunion would always be complex and passionate. The cat sulked. Anna had to work hard to win back her love, putting little dabs of tuna on the pad of her finger, which eventually the cat would lick off, accusingly. But she always forgives her cat, because this drama is not one-sided. The cat is reciprocal, shows empathy. Anna never feels taken advantage of. When the cat has abandoned Anna, she knows when it's time to come home, when it's time to curl up beside her because Anna needs her.

She phones Avery back.

'You sound tired,' says Avery.

'Tired. Defeated. These girls strip me back until all I have left are my own weaknesses and failings. They lever me open so casually. I know I'm the wrong person. I know the girls want Rachel, of course they do. Why should they feel grateful to me? This situation needs more strength than I ever knew I had. Giving when needed, knowing when to retreat, without being told. There is nothing more repellent to a child than a needy adult. I have to constantly read the signs, know when it's time to back off, or time to push forward. Offer them nothing but warmth, be the best replacement I can be; yet they don't want my warmth, or don't want to appear to want it, but still I have to give it, because they need it and will deeply resent me if it's not offered.' Anna dabs at her eyes with a tissue. She had no idea she was so upset. 'I made a cake with Isabella. I felt as if we were getting somewhere. But again, almost immediately, she vanishes. It's this constant process of needing and refusing. I mustn't require anything in return, take no offence if they reject me, but know instinctively when they need me and let it be known that I know. It's exhausting, Ave.'

'You're very brave, Anna.'

'I'm failing.'

'Then come home and get your cat. *She* will appreciate you.'

Anna laughs. 'I will,' she says.

When Avery hangs up, Anna carries on checking through her phone. A message from Andrew. He tried calling the landline, but couldn't get through. Could she phone him back? He'd really like to talk. Then a message from Jerri,

180

wondering how they're getting on. Before she calls her back, Anna ponders the question. How *are* they getting on? We are reverting to savages: I shat in a mud hole; the girls have a shrine and dance around a fire; I gaze at the stars and think about death. I'm realising the thinness of the line between sanity and insanity, that neither are fixed states; sanity is a privilege, insanity an inevitability in certain circumstances. But instead, Anna phones Jerri back, mentions the problems with the water, says the girls seem brighter, more engaged with the world, tells her that David is enjoying the change from London. The sea air seems to be good for his complexion. He looks younger, fresher. 'Oh, that's good news,' says Jerri. 'I was so worried about him.' She phones Andrew back but he's at work, he can't really talk. 'I'm coming home for a few nights,' she says. 'We'll go out for dinner together.'

Anna walks back to the house with an effervescent pain lodged within her solar plexus. Jittery, immediate, right on the surface. She could punch Brendan if she saw him, and she doesn't know exactly why.

It's six in the evening when Anna finally parks up outside her house. She made good progress because she rushed, stopping only once to refuel and buy a sandwich, but all this sitting has left her stiff. She stretches as she gets out of the car. Still dirty. No make-up. It's only here, once she's home, that she realises how far from her usual self she is. Scruffy and chaotic. She feels ashamed of herself. What if she sees one of the neighbours? Perhaps they'll telephone her, alerting her to the dirty, unwashed madwoman breaking into her home.

Once inside, though, she feels awash with calm. Her own place, her home; a house that doesn't fall apart if her gaze isn't constantly upon it. Even in this state, she feels familiar again to herself. She knows how to live in this house, because it looks after her, rather than the other way round, where the house expects her to do nothing but look after it.

The cat. There she is. A grey furry polka dot on her pillow. How could she have been so cruel as to have left her? The cat's head rises sleepily, but then she double-takes, holds Anna's gaze with her wide, almond-shaped glare. Her eyes are like hard, little emeralds, and they don't budge from Anna, even as Anna sits beside her to stroke her long fur. Tangled, because no one knew she needed to be combed regularly. She looks so unloved. No wonder the cat is cross. Anna runs her fingers through her fur, releasing some of the smaller knots. The cat purrs loudly, as if she's so helpless in her joy she can't find the means to be defiant or furious, even though Anna suspects she'd love to feel able to stalk out of the room, demand that Anna fight for her attention.

Eventually, it's the cat who moves first. Happily slipping off the bed, she disappears downstairs. Anna makes it into the bathroom, removing her dirty clothes, her second skin. In the shower, she lathers the soap, washing every inch, restoring herself. She dresses in fresh clothes, empties her suitcase into the washing machine, pours herself a gin and tonic. No lemon. Such bliss, to step out of the front door, walk up the road to the corner shop, buy a lemon, say hello to Serge as he takes her money, asks her where she's been. 'House-sitting,' she says.

'Lucky you,' he replies. 'Anywhere nice?'

Back at home, she and the cat are fully reunited. Curled up on her knee. 'I love you, and you love me,' Anna whispers into the cat's ear. It is only when she sees her handbag resting against the sofa that she remembers she hasn't called David. When she switches her phone on, there are three text messages from him. Can she let him know she's arrived? Then, ten minutes later: *Anna, are you OK? How's the journey going?* Then, almost immediately: *Let me know you are OK.* He sounds worried, so she calls him. It goes straight to voicemail. She leaves a message, then texts him to say she's fine.

She picks up the pile of letters Avery has stacked on the coffee table for her. When her mobile rings again, she briefly glances at it, assuming it will be David, but it's Andrew, he says he'll come over to have dinner with her straight away. Anna phones around to the restaurant on the corner, manages to get a table for two.

When Andrew arrives, he has cream-coloured paint streaks down the front of his shirt, tells Anna he took the day off to paint his sitting room. She wants to tell him to change, to fetch a clean shirt of David's from upstairs, but stops herself. He's a grown man. She must adapt. When they hug, her head barely reaches further than his chest. He feels like a giant, more like Peter than David.

Before they go out, she pours them both a drink and they sit down. Andrew drains his in one go, then gets up again to fetch himself another, sits back down, then gets up one more time, leans against the mantelpiece, the ice cubes rattling in his glass as he resists the urge to drain the second. It isn't until they are seated in the restaurant with a bottle of wine and two plates of the day's homemade pasta with mushroom and truffle sauce that Anna says, 'Andrew, you're drinking an awful lot.'

'Am I?'

Anna says nothing, waits for him to fill the silence.

'I'm feeling pressured. I'm painting the flat. Jessica wants to move in. I went to her parents' house at the weekend. They were all looking at me expectantly, as if they're anticipating me delivering something, providing them all with a service they can't directly ask for, but absolutely believe it's my duty to impart. It's terrifying.'

'Poor you,' Anna says.

He pulls at the neck of his shirt. 'I feel suffocated. At night, my entire body itches. I can't settle.'

'You don't have to do anything you don't feel ready to do,' Anna says.

'The whole world has all these expectations.'

'Not me and your father. You won't let us down.'

'I'm worried about life,' says Andrew, in a way that

makes Anna remember him as an earnest eleven-year-old boy.

'I think you're upset by Rachel and Peter,' Anna says.

'I want to enjoy myself, have fun.'

'You don't have to marry Jessica tomorrow.'

They continue talking, Anna trying to gently reassure him, he thinking out loud about whether or not he wants to find someone wilder, more on the edge? He feels that marriage is the end.

'The end of what?' Anna asks.

Andrew pauses. 'The end of life.'

'I like Jessica,' says Anna.

'So do I, but . . .'

They finish eating, ask for the bill. Anna goes to pay out of habit, but Andrew scoops the bill out of her hand. He'll pay. Anna relinquishes it, adopting her newly passive role. The waiter takes his card, puts it through the machine. Andrew enters his PIN. Anna thinks how grown up he is. Of course he's grown up. What else would he be? She takes her scarf from the back of the chair. They head out into the cold night, a five-minute walk home. Andrew decides to stay the night in his old bed. He pours them each a brandy; they settle into chairs. Anna puts a log on the fire, and Andrew keeps probing her. He wants to know about her life, her marriage. Has she ever thought about other men? It takes Anna a long time to answer before she says: yes. Yes, she has thought about other men; most women have. Not often though, she adds, when she sees the look on his face.

'Who?' Andrew asks.

Anna tells him about a curator she met at a Rothko exhibition. She liked him; they talked on the steps of the Tate until long after the gallery closed. Before they parted, he asked for her phone number. She knew she shouldn't give it to him, but she did anyway. Then she found herself thinking about him almost constantly, hoping he would call, but couldn't understand why she felt that way. She had everything she wanted with David, yet desire for this other man lodged in her chest like a pain. Andrew listens. Anna is surprised by his lack of resistance to this story. He never asks her to stop, even though she wonders if she ought to be telling him.

'He did call, and we went for lunch together. He showed me pictures of an exhibition he was organising on technology and its influence on painting. In another life, I could have married someone like him. We were interested in the same things. He liked art and reading.'

Andrew stays quiet, lets her continue.

'I still love your father,' she says. 'But the thing that is difficult for any man to understand is that for women with young children, it feels like your life has been broken into pieces, whereas for a man, their life remains whole. I often felt jealous of your father as I tried to fit these small pieces of myself together to make a whole shape, while he had to do nothing of the sort. I was always rearranging these pieces, trying to make a whole, never succeeding; starting over, arranging and rearranging, while his life carried on as normal. For that lunch with the curator, for those two hours, I felt like a whole person. I wasn't patched together. I was an actual grown woman, an adult, sitting opposite someone who could see me. I wasn't having to shore myself up.'

'Did you do anything with him?'

'A kiss. A brief kiss. We walked through an underpass together and he took my hand, asked if it was just him who felt this thing. I said "No," and we kissed. When I got home, the whole thing made me feel like a stranger to myself, a stranger within my life, an enemy to your father, and so I didn't see him again.' She turns to Andrew, smiling. 'Although I could have brought him home while Dad was at work and had all the sex I wanted with him.'

'Mum! That's disgusting.'

'I'm teasing you, Andrew. I didn't do it. I'm saying I could have done it, but I didn't, because I loved your father.'

'What about Dad?' says Andrew. 'Has he thought about other women?'

'You'd have to ask him,' she replies. She won't say more than that, even though, at the very front of her mind as she told Andrew this story, was the thought that she had wanted to take the curator to bed out of revenge, because years before all that, she'd found a receipt in David's trousers pocket for a bunch of flowers. At the time, she'd sat on the bed and sobbed at the brutal inevitability of it all. She was tired, struggling; she'd only just had Matthew.

When David came home, she flung the receipt at him. It fluttered to the floor between them. David looked bewildered, then picked it up. A frightened look of recognition came over him. He confessed immediately. It was his secretary. Yes, he was attracted to her, she flirted with him, he'd bought her flowers, but nothing had happened. A vague fantasy he caught in time, nothing real. But, several years later, Anna saw that secretary at a Christmas drinks party. The woman – although she seemed little more than a girl – swished between the different guests without any knowledge of Anna's hard stare. She wore a silky dark-blue dress with gold earrings. She was attractive, very attractive. She seemed to hold the room in the palm of her hand.

'That's her, isn't it?' Anna had said to David.

It took him a moment to understand what she meant. 'She doesn't work in the department any more,' he'd replied.

Anna didn't trust his reply. It was too glib, too easy, too quick off the tongue, as if he'd known this woman and Anna might meet, so had practised what he would say. Anna observed the studied way David and this woman ignored each other. It was more than a bunch of flowers, or they would have spoken. Anna's most vivid memory of that evening was how lonely she felt. Standing completely still in the middle of the party, she watched all the other couples. She wondered if everyone else's marriages felt to them like being marooned on an island. Had they all walked through a door that had banged shut behind them?

'The thing you must remember, Andrew,' Anna says, 'is that whatever you decide with Jessica, or with anyone else, there will be a moment, or frequent moments, in any marriage when you believe it is over. There's nothing to be done, you can't stand that person, you can't repair it, don't want to repair it – you hate them. And then it passes, and the next moment you're in love again. You mustn't let those moments confuse you. You must ride them out. This moment you're experiencing now with Jessica – the boredom, the fury, the disgust, whatever it is – it will change into something else, and you'll love each other again.'

'And if it doesn't?'

'It usually does. It usually changes.'

'It just sounds so horribly bourgeois. All the sacrifice. And for what?'

'It's called being an adult,' replies Anna. 'It happens to everyone eventually.'

Andrew falls silent. They stare at the fire. Drink another brandy.

'How is Dad?' asks Andrew eventually.

'He's fine,' says Anna. 'He's coping well, considering.'

Anna feels restored as she returns to Scotland. In the end, she'd stayed in London for a week. She helped Andrew to finish painting his flat. Refugees from their lives, they spent their evenings eating Indian takeaways in front of the fire, drinking too much wine, then stayed in bed until late into the morning. It was so good that when it came time to leave, Anna was tearful. Andrew rolled his eyes – said he hated it when she got needy. Patiently, he coaxed her into the car. She sensed he was ready for her to go. She spent a night in Cumbria on the drive back up.

It's still daylight when she arrives back at the house. The air feels pure and crisp. No wind. The sea barely moves. The sky is a magnifying glass, refracting the thin winter sunlight. Anna takes the cat's box from the front seat, sets it down on the gravel, opens the door. 'It's chilly up here,' she whispers. 'Much chillier than you're used to.' The cat doesn't move. She cowers at the back of the box, staring at Anna with round, terrified eyes. Anna strokes her nose. 'Come on,' she coaxes. 'There's mice and birds, rats, squirrels. You'll find all sorts up here.'

Still, the cat stares back at her. Anna closes the lid. She knows the steps to this particular dance. In the kitchen, she tries again. She tickles the cat's ears, opens a tin of tuna. Still the cat cowers at the back, so she tries folding a blanket close to the fire and showing it to the cat. Look! A nice cosy bed in the best spot, catching all the warmth! Still, the cat won't move. There's nothing more to be done for her. Anna leaves a saucer of milk by the open box and abandons her. If she's going to be like that, then what does she expect?

At the bottom of the stairs, Anna calls out. Is anyone home? No response. Upstairs, there's no one. Only a trail of clothes running from the bathroom to the girls' bedroom, where they must have been flung off and forgotten. She picks them up, hangs them over a chair. Inside the bedroom, sofa cushions are arranged on the floor. Next to them, a pair of man's brown socks.

When Anna comes downstairs, the cat has relented. She is lapping the milk. Anna kisses her behind the ears. The cat stops drinking, looks up at her mistress – what is it in those eyes? Love? Impotence? Fury? – then returns to her milk. Anna wants to fill the kettle, but only brown water splutters from the tap, then a low, deep groan. The plumbing. She'd forgotten. She searches for bottles of water, but finds only empties.

Back in the car, she speeds off to the local shop. It closes at lunchtime, but she might just get there. As she arrives, the woman is rolling down the metal shutters. Anna waves at her. Will she open up again for just five minutes? The woman ignores her, even though Anna is certain she can see her. Bitch! She starts the car once again, heads to the port – but, even there, everything is closed. The whole place closed by Saturday lunchtime. Anna abandons her search, returns to the house to find David and Brendan unloading bags of shopping.

'I wasn't expecting you until much later,' says David, hugging her. 'We bought fish at the docks. We planned on cooking for you.'

'The plumber didn't come yet?' Anna says.

'He did,' replies David. 'He's stabilised it. He's coming back tomorrow.'

The cat threads through Anna's legs, purring loudly, until finally she achieves the thing she intends: David

191

notices her. 'You brought her back,' he says, picking Sammy up with one hand, kissing her behind her ears. The cat purrs ever louder. David takes her off to show the girls.

The next morning, Brendan and David are working at the shrine, making a white canvas lean-to. Inside it, they stack logs, but they have to work twice as hard because the wind is fighting them. Eventually, stacking complete, they boil a kettle on the gas stove, make mugs of tea. Brendan tips out his dregs on to the grass, then scales the outside of the shrine. He's like a cat, climbing the walls, pulling on the joints, checking everything is secure. While he's busy, David unloads the rest of the things from the back of the tractor. Anna squints to get a better view: pillows, another mattress, duvets, blankets. David dumps them inside the shrine, then returns to bring in gloves, coats, hats, more firewood.

They return to the house to find Anna. 'Now don't be cross, Anna, but you won't see David for a few days,' says Brendan.

'I'm going to stay a couple of nights in the shrine,' David says.

'An experiment with the wilderness,' says Brendan. 'Such things are good for men.'

David looks embarrassed, interrupts Brendan. 'I just want some time to be alone, to reflect, in nature,' he says.

'We don't want you to get cross,' says Brendan.

'So, what is this?' asks Anna.

'He's having an elemental experience.'

'With a duvet?' she snaps.

'Anna, please don't be cross,' says David.

'He's going to spend three days and three nights in the wild. He has the shrine for shelter, fresh water, a good supply of wood for a fire. He's got one of Peter's guns to have a go at a rabbit, as well as a fishing rod. He's going to light fires, sleep under the stars and hunt. It'll do him the world of good,' says Brendan, cheerily.

'I do need it,' mutters David. 'I haven't felt—'

'David's been through a lot,' interrupts Brendan.

Anna would like to smack Brendan. How patronising! Who is he to tell her what kind of a state her husband is in?

'I've always wanted to do something like this,' says David. 'And now, more than ever, I need peace and solitude.'

'Is there not already enough peace and solitude in the house?'

David doesn't answer. He eats his lunch, then gathers up more warm coats, extra blankets, and leaves. She stands at the kitchen window as he tramples down to the shrine, carrying his pile of stuff. Once there, he opens the door and disappears from view. Gone.

And so it begins.

That night, she clambers into her cold little bed alone. The next morning, first thing, before anything else, she checks the shrine from the upstairs window. A trail of smoke, a fire, then David, wrapped up in a duvet, sitting on a log, hunched over, holding a tin mug. A miserable scene.

The girls are still asleep. Brendan is reading in the library. With nothing to occupy her, Anna drives to the ferry, rides it to the neighbouring island, from where she takes another ferry to the mainland. She drives until she comes across a pretty town with a café. She orders at the counter, a pot of tea. A young girl serves her, barely older than Sasha and Isabella. Her glance doesn't wander upwards to Anna's unwashed hair, or downwards to her filthy fingernails. Surely, she smells. But Anna, this grubby person, falling apart at the seams, attracts no comment, not even a sideways glance, and for that, she's grateful. Invisibility, for once, feels like a liberation. The girl takes Anna's cash, pings open the till. Before Anna has even had time to pick up her tea, the cashier is moving on to the person behind her.

She finds a seat at a table for two. The emptiness of the seat opposite weighs on her. She'd like it to be filled – not with Avery, or another friend, but with someone she doesn't know. Someone a little older than herself, but who would understand her situation. She'd like to tell this fantasy friend: my husband has gone mad. He's in the wilderness, because he'd like to feel elemental. He wants to find his inner wolf. Six months ago, he was a shipping lawyer in London. He went to work in crisp, pressed shirts and gold monogrammed cufflinks, worked hard for his promotions. Now he's a hunter-gatherer, sleeping in a hut with a gun to shoot his dinner. Her fantasy friend will tell Anna that she, too, had a husband who went mad for a time, but he recovered. It's his age, she'll say. He's at a difficult moment in his life. He's seeing an abyss, a dread, that he can't quite put a name to: men do go weird at his age, she'll say. Be thankful it's not something worse than being a wolf for three nights.

Too much thinking turns you into a mad woman. Anna would like to be a sane woman – they can't all lose their heads – so she finishes her tea, walks back through the street towards her car. As she searches for the key in her bag, she checks her phone. A message from Andrew: could she call him as soon as she gets it?

Back at the house, Brendan pours Anna a glass of wine. The girls drift into the kitchen, tell Anna they're not hungry and go to their bedroom, so Anna and Brendan take their drinks through to the library, where Brendan lights the fire.

'I'm so worried. I really should drive home,' says Anna. 'But then I can't leave David up here in this state.'

'It'll be the making of him,' Brendan says.

'I really should get David. He'd want to know.'

'It can wait a day or two.'

'Why would a young man do that to his life?'

Anna drinks the wine quickly, holds her glass out for more. The alcohol is helping. She tells Brendan how Andrew and Jessica first met – on the Tube, of all places. When Andrew introduced his mother to Jessica, they liked each other instantly. They talked all evening. It felt to Anna as if she finally had a daughter. Just the right kind of woman for

Andrew. Her third glass of wine. Brendan throws another log on the fire.

'Andrew expressed some doubts. Nothing unusual, nothing I wouldn't expect at the brink of making such a big decision. I had no inkling he was just going to put a bomb under everything and walk away.'

'He is very young,' Brendan replies.

'David and I were married at twenty-six,' Anna says. 'We didn't feel too young. Quite the opposite; it felt like an adventure. Setting up home together. Taking on a new role in life.'

'But these days, it's different.'

'I could understand it if he wanted to have some fun. But leaving his job? Renting out his flat? Going travelling? He's twenty-six, not eighteen. He should have done this years ago.'

'I admire him,' says Brendan. He holds up his glass to Anna.

'Well of course *you* do,' says Anna. Brendan laughs. He clinks his glass against hers, which makes Anna laugh. They talk about marriage, about Andrew, and what all this will mean for the future – will she ever be a grandmother? – and Anna enjoys talking to him, likes hearing his perspective. For a moment, loosened by the wine, she forgets how tiresome she's been finding him. There are good things about him – of course there are – because they've been friends for over thirty years. Andrew will be fine, he says. David too. For this reassurance, she is grateful. She feels better.

They don't have dinner. Instead they pick at some cheese, open a bottle of red wine. Brendan suggests they sit closer to the fire. Anna pauses at the window to see if she can spot David, but there is nothing. No lights, no fire: nothing.

'He'll be fine,' Brendan says. 'Stop worrying. He said if it got too much, he would come home. There's no pressure.'

'He'll die of exposure.'

'No, he won't. He'll live with renewed vigour. Why do you always see everything in negative terms?'

They are both on the hearth, close to the fire. Anna hugs her knees into her chest. Brendan pokes at the logs. Brendan must have fetched another bottle of wine, because Anna notices that the bottle seems full, and they've already had three glasses each. It feels good to drink. How stressed she's felt. The wine is good. Brendan is making her laugh. Just the thing she needs.

'When's this plumber going to come?' Anna asks.

Brendan laughs. 'You feeling ripe?'

'I need to wash.'

Brendan sniffs his own armpits. 'I'm not too bad,' he says.

'I do hope Andrew's doing the right thing,' says Anna.

'Of course he is,' says Brendan.

'I thought Jessica was right for him. Andrew needs someone like her. Someone stable. He'll be all over the place if he meets a woman who's too much like he is.'

'It's a question of perspective, the way we give meaning

to things, the way our own arbitrary cultural system is—'

'Oh, stop bloody preaching,' says Anna.

They laugh. They're both drunk now. Everything seems funny. Nothing matters. Anna lies back on the rug.

'It's just very dull. This life path,' says Brendan.

'It's the path I took.'

Brendan shrugs.

'You think I'm boring?'

'You're very middle class.'

'That's not a compliment, coming from you.'

'It's just a thing. I never judge.'

'Yes, you do,' says Anna. 'You're the most judgemental person I know.'

Brendan laughs.

'No, really. The thing you can't understand, Brendan, is that the things I value most of all are family and home. You feel contempt for women like me. For bourgeois women. Boring little fucking housewives who can't see through the system the way you can.'

Brendan is leaning back on his elbow, face cupped in his hand. His eyebrow is raised. Is he amused? Or surprised? He is looking at Anna in that same way he looked at her when they first met at the party all those years ago, when she was a little stiff, wearing her favourite silk scarf, and he was louche in a dirty leather jacket, smoking a roll-up. A look of wry amusement, like a shark playing with its prey, because the darker part of him enjoys the feeling of power it gives him.

'Who said anything about contempt?' says Brendan.

This response irritates Anna. She raises her voice, to make her point. 'The reason David and I are here in this house is because of everyone's belief that David and I were the only couple stable enough to provide a home for the girls. Stable, calm, kind people, able to help them make sense of the world again.'

'I never said I felt contempt for you, Anna,' says Brendan.

Anna finds herself standing up, her voice rising. 'You need a woman like me who can tidy a bedroom, wash sheets, put a pan of soup on the stove, make a fruit cake, go to the supermarket, put milk in the fridge, bread on the table, do everything required to make a home feel ordered.' Anna is shouting now, her finger thumping her chest. '*I'm* the one who's ensured the beds are clean. *I'm* the one who's made sure food is always available. Washed the towels, washed the clothes, cleaned up the vomit, and yet the girls look at me as if I'm nothing. A housewife. *I hope we'll never be you*, their looks say to me. You know, Brendan, sometimes I hate them. No one gives a fuck how I feel about doing all of this. It's not just the girls. You've all treated me with contempt.'

'Anna, we've all been hard at work,' Brendan says, calmly. 'You're drunk. I don't think I've ever seen you drunk before.'

'I'm not.'

'But this is the thing I find so troublesome about feminism. All this you're saying to me: it's one-sided. It's self-centred. It fails to identify that everyone's fucked. For every poor, hard-done-by woman, there's some tired, downtrodden bastard doing a job he fucking hates. A man with his soul in tatters. Patriarchy fucks us all, Anna. While you were in London, flowering-arranging and shopping and fucking about organising lunch parties and swimming lessons, David was in the City, being demeaned by an inhumane corporate structure in order to pay for it all.'

'Brendan. What the fuck do you know about feminism?' she says. 'David had a choice.'

'As do you, Anna. You've always had a choice. You're not a child. You chose this life for yourself. Pursued it, in fact. You're not a victim. You colluded with David in this bourgeois dream, and now you're blaming him for your unhappiness.'

'I'm not unhappy,' snaps Anna.

Brendan moves towards her. His hot breath is on her cheek. 'I know – I just know – that you've imagined a different kind of life. A different kind of self.'

'No,' says Anna, tersely. 'I haven't. You're mistaken.'

'A life like mine.'

'No chance.'

'A life of freedom. You've never imagined falling asleep in different arms? A pair of dark, muscular arms? On the other side of the world, drifting off to the sound of fat, tropical raindrops falling on fat, tropical leaves. Wandering through a labyrinth of candlelit corridors to a room heady with the smell of incense, with a young male masseur barely visible in the flickering light. Rubbing musk oil on to you. A man who'll gaze at your naked body as if you were the first woman he's ever beheld.'

Brendan is up close to her. He's so naff. His hot breath tickles the insides of her ear. 'I know you have a fantasy about being far away, living at the edge, because you've spent your life living so far *from* the edge. I know all this,' says Brendan, 'because people – women – confide in me. Particularly the married ones. You're in exactly the same state as David is. You've had to give up just as much as he has. You're just better at hiding it.'

Anna wants to cry but stops herself. She's too angry. Brendan will not reduce her to a whimpering child. 'I have worked very hard for my life,' she snaps. 'It's not worth nothing. We need all these structures that you find so intolerable in order to manage. We need order to live. And Andrew is very foolish to throw it all away.' Anna slams down her wine, heads towards the door, all the time yelling drunkenly that we all need order, even him.

'No. I'm like all men, I just need a little cunt from time to time to keep me happy,' says Brendan, smiling at her in such a way that Anna feels seized by something.

She runs towards him, grabs at him. Driven by a force she can't explain, she yanks a clump of his hair, holds it tight in her hand so she can pull his head, jerk it right and left. Oh, this feeling of power over him! He yells. Tells her she's mad. Get a grip of yourself! With her other hand, she slaps his face – his sweaty, stubbly, red face. He is flailing, trying to grab her hand any way he can. His face reddens even more. He's salivating with rage. Little blobs of it at the corners of his mouth. Anna wants to tear him apart, to rip his head off.

'You wanted us all to become savages,' she says. 'Isn't this what savages do? They fight.' Her foot sinks into the flesh of his thigh. He yelps, but it gives him an advantage. He grabs her leg, flips her on to the floor, felling her with a force that brings her to her senses. Anna sits up, brushes her hair flat again, catches her breath. Heat ripples through her body. The shame. She runs from the room.

Upstairs, she throws herself on to the bed. Brendan always makes her feel so small, so conservative. She ends up saying things she doesn't even believe in. She did try to fire up her sons' imaginations. She didn't want them to only learn facts, only develop skills. She wants Andrew to be happy, more than anything. Brendan reduces everything, brings everything down to sex. He's such a fool, an idiot. Of course she knows that life is complicated. What does he take her for? She feels herself shake. All the things she believes in, all the things she holds dear, Brendan takes pleasure in dismantling. Anna lies on the bed, tries to stop thinking about him, his ideas. Somehow, Brendan phrases things in such a way she can never find a response. She can't find a way to really prove him wrong. Anna takes long, slow breaths to calm herself. 'I like the way I am. I like the way I am,' she whispers to herself.

She gets up to close the shutters. She's dizzy. She staggers back to the bed to lie, cocooned by the dark, hiding from the large mirror, and the photographs of Rachel on the wall opposite the bed. Rachel stares at her every morning. The first thing she sees when she opens her eyes. The same way those two girls look at her. The same way Brendan does. She's tired of being looked at, of shifting each time she's placed in someone's gaze, each with their own ideas about what they will find in her. She wants to hide in the dark, where no one can find her, no one can define her.

She has drunk too much. She feels awful. Brendan's words are still swimming inside her. The more she tries to ignore them, the louder they force their way in. And, in fact, he's wrong about women. Who are these women he's been talking to? Her sexual longings aren't those of soft-porn movies, dark men dressed up in gold kaftans holding a bottle of massage oil. The thing she lacks, the thing she's never experienced, the thing she longs for, is the violence of erotic love. Her lovemaking with David is amiable enough, companionable and predictable – no less satisfying for it – but they don't throw each other around the room. They don't *have* to have one another. They choose to have one another, because sex is what you do in a marriage. She isn't longing for candles and musk oil and Ali Baba: she just wants to get properly fucked.

Anna runs her hands through her hair. One hand falls on to her breast. She moves it further down her body until it rests at the top of her trousers. She unbuttons them,

203

pushes her hand inwards, into her underwear. She hasn't washed for days, since she was in Cumbria. She feels sticky. She couldn't have sex with David, or anyone else, in this state anyway. Smelling like this, she'd be ashamed. Her fingers slip further inside herself. She feels a private contentment. Her head spins with the alcohol. The movement of her hand makes her feel dizzier. At the end of the bed, the cat is curled into a tight coil of soft, warm fur. She rubs more and more quickly, her body stiffening, keeping going until the orgasm rushes through her body, all the way through her legs, torso, arms and up to her head. A deep, private pleasure. Her legs fall against the bed, the feelings still flickering through her body like small, intense electric shocks. She relaxes, flooded with warmth. Soon after, she falls asleep.

When Anna awakes, it's still the middle of the night. She's fully clothed. The cold makes her feel ill. She gets up to peek through the shutters. By the sea, there is the faint flicker of a fire. She no longer feels cross with David. She just wants him to come inside, for them all to go home, for this madness to stop. She wants to put David in the car, drive him back to London. They could have their sons over for Sunday lunch. She and Avery could go to the theatre together. They could wander up the road to the local wine bar, spend an evening talking with whoever else happened to be there. Then David would go to work and she'd look after the house, then look after him when he came in from the office, and she wouldn't give a shit what Brendan, or younger women, or anyone else thought of this old-fashioned arrangement, because David also looks after her: it's reciprocal. She isn't a doormat. Brendan would go back to being the person who phoned them occasionally, came over for dinner every now and again. He would be contained, his ideas muted, within the ordinary routines of their life. At their dinner parties, he'd play the role of fool, of jester, livening up a boring evening. He'd be the man all the other men were glad not to be, but they'd laugh, all the same, at his antics. He wouldn't have the power to disrupt Anna and David.

Up here, the problem is one of perspective. Without their friends dropping in or their two sons coming for lunch, there's nothing to divert them. Their minds seem to bend and refract the isolation around them. They each bring out the worst in the other, until there is no clear sense of the things that are important, the things that are normal.

She must have fallen back to sleep, because when she awakes again, it's daytime. She checks on the girls. Still asleep so she goes downstairs to find Brendan crunching through wholemeal toast and butter at the kitchen table.

At the sight of her, he immediately moves towards her, takes her hand. 'Anna, I'm sorry. I was a dick last night. A complete dick. It was all my fault. Everything. I'm sorry. I was totally out of order. It was wrong of me. I don't know what came over me. I think I must have lost my tolerance for booze. I was horrible. I'd like to blame it on the drink. I was horribly drunk. And I was horrible to you.'

Brendan insists on making her some tea. Would she like some toast? 'It was cruel of me,' he continues. 'I was cruel to you, and I'm sorry for that. Cruelty should not be my thing. I don't like to think of myself as cruel or vicious – I suppose we can all be cruel and vicious at times – but I should never have spoken to you like that. I was drunk. And I didn't mean the things I said.'

Anna no longer cares enough to protest. She sits down to eat the toast he's made. He finishes his tea, pours her a mug and sighs. 'It's just been such an intense time. For me too. For all of us. I've realised so much.' He pauses while he finishes munching his toast. 'Anna, I'm not happy. I'm thinking of winding down my teaching. I no longer know who I am or what I want.'

Anna wants Brendan to stop talking.

'I'm lost. Do I even have a future? I think it's why I was such an idiot to you last night. I'm wondering if me, my life, has been totally pointless. I need to do something meaningful. Even just one worthwhile thing.' Brendan stands up from his chair, paces the room. 'What we need is a return to something.' He turns to Anna, looking her straight in the eye. 'Perhaps this place, these girls, this house: we could set something up. We could get people coming up here to get in touch with this side of themselves. We could give them a week, a weekend, whatever it is, to get them to connect with this thing we've all lost, that we need to reconnect with. This house would be perfect for that. We can light fires outdoors, the sea, the foraging, the woods. We can build things, have spiritual festivals and evenings. We could come to a financial arrangement with the girls. That way, they get to stay here, the house pays for itself, we get to do something truly original and revolutionary. We need to pull apart the structures of our mad world and look underneath them. We wouldn't need to make money. We'd just need to survive; and help others to survive this world. People could make donations.'

'No,' says Anna.

'I can tell I'm irritating you, but this place has been good for you too. You've been a part of this, a part of what we've been doing. You've been processing like mad since you've been here, Anna. And I've achieved something with those girls. Don't just dismiss me, without considering it.'

Anna says nothing.

'I feel desperate, Anna. Come on. Please help me.'

'What's Uncle David doing?' asks Isabella.

'No idea,' snaps Anna with such force that Isabella looks hurt. 'It's not you,' she adds, softening. 'I'm just very cross with Uncle David. For being so damn selfish.'

Again, Isabella startles as if this glimpse of the fragility of the very world that is supposed to be holding together her own fragile world is too much to bear. Anna watches the child retreat, no doubt confused. She feels guilty. This is all David's fault. Outrage builds within her until finally she cracks. She marches down to the shrine to put a stop to this nonsense once and for all. But when she gets there, she can't find David. She can only see the evidence of him. The embers of a fire, a mug lying on its side, a used teabag nestling among the blades of grass. Anna steps inside the shrine. Duvets, sleeping bags, a pile of blankets, bottles of water. She spots Peter's gun leaning up against the wall. Outside, a ladder is set against the wall. She climbs it, on to the roof, and there he is. Lying, covered in blankets, staring up at the sky. He doesn't see her. She watches him. The clouds drift above him. Eventually, she whispers, 'David.'

He jumps. 'What are you doing here?'

'I made you a sandwich and some hot tea.'

He sits up, disorientated.

'What are you doing?' Anna asks.

'I'm lying very still, staring at the sky.'

Anna doesn't know what to say. She stands there, holding the plastic bag containing the sandwich and the tea.

'Anna. I'm supposed to be staying alone.'

'Why don't you just come inside? You must be freezing.'

'Please, Anna,' he says. 'Let me do this.'

'What is it achieving?'

'Leave me alone,' David hisses. 'You're so needy.'

Shocked, Anna retreats to the house but by evening, she's had enough. She creeps out the back door, picks her way down to the shrine by torchlight. She sweeps her torch around, sees the empty flask, the box without her sandwich in it. David is sitting outside, a fire lit, sparks drifting off into the cold air.

'David, I've had enough of this now,' says Anna. She says it crossly, to let him know that it really is time for him to stop.

'If I lie very still, and stare up at the clouds, I feel calm.'

Anna holds the torch more firmly in her hand. Something in the blankness of David's face worries her.

'I want out of all this,' he says.

Anna says nothing.

'Of this life. Of work.'

'Because of Peter?'

'I want to be alone.'

'What?'

'I've been thinking about it for months. I want a divorce.'

'Do you have someone else?'

'Something internal is compelling me to be alone,' he says.

In her room, Anna lies on her bed. An empty space beside her. Her body no longer feels like her own. She's shifted into unfamiliar territory. Opposite her, Rachel is still diving through the air, without a care in the world. Does David even know what he is asking for? Can Anna just return to London alone?

That night, she sleeps fitfully. She wakes continually until the first light keeps her awake. An image from her dream sits inside her head, refuses to go away: a child's toe poking up from the earth. The soft blue chill of dawn is just beginning. Ribbons of pink across the sky. The beauty and benevolence of the morning sky do nothing to quell the image in her head. The dream makes her feel sick. She can't shake it off. How can she and David fail so spectacularly after a life with so little discordance? She's tolerated so much with David. She allowed him to be himself. And who is she? The woman who made their life the way it is. Anna is muttering the words. *This is who I am. The woman who did everything. This is who I am.* All that she has done, and then he takes this last thing for himself, too. Unfulfilled? Whose fault is that? He had every chance to be fulfilled.

When she finally manages to dress and go downstairs, the house is in silence. She checks at the window. No sign of a fire. Is he enjoying the deep slumber of the recently liberated? Is he full of relief? Finally – finally! – he had the courage to say the thing he really felt. She turns her back to the window to better observe herself within her new identity. The rejected woman is making her tea. Now she is spreading butter on a half piece of toast. Her appetite won't tolerate the whole of it. She nibbles. Even the act of eating feels tentative now. Her instinct is to call her sons, to announce the news to them: look at what your father has done to me, and after everything I did for him. She'd like to do it before David has the chance to speak to them. What if he convinces them that she has failed him? Whereas if Anna calls the boys first, she'll control the narrative. Hers would be the official version. David would only ever hold the secondary position of arguing against the story she created. She would weaken him, strengthen herself. She needs to gather an army, start phoning around, whip their friends up into outrage so they'll take her side. Manipulative? Perhaps. But she's not a nasty person. It's David who's been nasty. And anyway, it's not bullying if he deserves it. Her phone sits on the table. It's a clear day. She could walk up to the cairn, beam out to the world her version of events. She's been wronged. She was the waitress at the banquet of her husband's life, and now she's been cruelly discarded. Who wouldn't sympathise with the woman in that story? But their private, enclosed world will be torn open for examination by others. And what if she can't convince them all? What if they think she is the one who failed?

A wash, this is what she needs. Upstairs, she packs some things into a bag: toothbrush, shampoo, clean clothes, underwear, make-up, body lotion. Downstairs, she takes the car keys, puts the bag on the front seat, drives to find a public swimming pool, a gym, anywhere she can wash herself. She'll head to the ferry, go to the mainland. As soon as her phone works, she'll be able to find a place. She checks her watch. She's been driving for forty-five minutes, still no ferry. She reverses the car, backs into a track, turns. She's lost. She's not concentrating. She heads down a narrow lane, then spots a group of people gathered outside a tiny whitewashed church. Sunday morning. Anna parks the car, walks towards it, drawn by the thought of being somewhere calm, a place with people, with sunlight streaming through the stained-glass windows, flecking her with patterns of miracles and unity. Anna ducks under an oak arch, crunches up the white gravel path, through the thick stone doorway. The sound of the organ ushers her inside, into the coolness of the stone interior. In the church, she feels instantly calm, protected. She sits tentatively at the very end of a pew. People glance in her direction. She avoids their gazes by fiddling with the hymn book. She doesn't want to be asked any questions. The organ music picks up force. The choir starts to sing, a sound so crystal clear and heartfelt Anna can't contain herself any longer. The song weakens her. She unhooks the cushion hanging on the back of the pew, drops to her knees. Holding her hands to her face, she closes her eyes. The thing that comes to her doesn't make sense. Only a feeling, no words: an emotion that colonises her, but she can neither understand nor articulate it. Words would make her feel safe, but they don't come. This feeling rises within her, the force of it gathers, presses as it searches for its escape route. It suffocates her. Green lights dance across her vision. The organ music crescendos into something melancholic, strangely joyful, the words of a choir imploring love, peace, joy, beauty. She holds her hands tight to her face, embarrassed at her total lack of control. Her whole body shakes. Can anyone see her? The tone of the music, the words of the songs, talking of pure, universal love, something untainted and singular. The feeling of it, its presence, completely undoes her. Her head and body swim with sadness and longing, she lost within it, until the vicar declares the service finished, forcing Anna to sit up. The light shocks her eyes. She blinks, as if coming round from a long sleep, notices the heads turned in her direction, staring at her. Was she so loud? She runs out of the church, fumbles at the gate to unlock it. A hand reaches out, calmly unlatches it for her. The other hand of this kind stranger squeezes her wrist. She can't bring herself to lift her face to see who it is, or even to thank them. Instead, she swings the gate open and runs to her car.

Anna eventually finds her way to the ferry, eyes swollen, mopping at her face. On the mainland, she follows signs to a leisure centre just off the bypass. She parks the car, negotiates an entrance fee with the woman at the turnstile – they usually only accept members – and stands under the heat and force of the shower. Cleansed, restored, wearing clean clothes, and with clean hair – styled with the help of a hairdryer she had to feed fifty pence pieces to – she drives back to the house, to wait for the man she thought was her husband to emerge from the wilderness.

the hunted

THE GIRLS WATCH AS DAVID AND ANNA LOAD A SMALL overnight bag into the boot of the car, telling them they'll be back tomorrow. Sasha asks where they're going.

'David and I just need to do something,' Anna replies.

'What do you have to do?' asks Isabella.

But they don't give her an answer. Instead, they close the lid of the boot, step into the car and drive off.

'You've got me all to yourselves,' Brendan says, grinning at them.

The gun room has two doors. The first, a normal cupboard door that forms a ruse for a second, heavier door set into a solid stone surround and bolted shut with a series of sturdy padlocks. Brendan works his way through the padlocks, releasing them all. Inside, guns are lined up against the wall. Opposite are shelves stacked with boxes of rounds, ropes, hunting knives, leatherbound notebooks holding records of previous shoots. Brendan picks out a rifle, a length of rope, a single box of rounds. He hesitates over the hunting knife, picks it up, puts it back, then: 'Yes, actually we will need a hunting knife,' he says. He slips it into his belt along with a second, smaller knife. He locks the door, returns the key to Peter's bedside drawer, while the girls wait.

'Now are you going to stop being sulky with me and just enjoy the day?' says Brendan to Isabella, carrying the guns.

'I'm not being sulky,' retorts Isabella.

Outside the light is sharp, hard-edged. Perfect for shooting, says Brendan, as he slings the gun over his shoulder, hangs the coil of rope around his neck, dumps the rounds into the deep pockets of his wax jacket. He heads off in the direction of the hill with the girls following, stumbling to keep up with him. Sasha falls behind them. She doesn't want to go. It's cruel. Red deer are beautiful: why would anyone want to kill them?

'Don't be such a wimp!' says Isabella, glancing up at Brendan. He looks pleased with her so she carries on. 'You're not a vegetarian. They're pests, anyway.'

They've been walking for ten minutes when Brendan spots something. Isabella squints to get a closer look, tells him they can't pursue it – 'It's not the season for males,' she says – and so they carry on, until it's Sasha who spots the female. The moment she tells everyone, she wishes she'd kept quiet, because the animal becomes their target. They watch her as she grazes. She looks up to chew, then her head drops again to tug at the grass. She begins wandering

215

up the hill. Sasha, Isabella and Brendan follow, crouching low to avoid being seen. Wherever the deer goes, they follow. Gradually, painstakingly, they begin to close in on her until it seems as if she's seen them – she looks in their direction with startled eyes – so the three of them remain very still.

They let her gain ground, become complacent once more. When she's no longer suspicious, they move again until they find the dry bed of an old stream. A useful place to hide. They jump down into it, drop to their bellies and crawl as quickly as they can along the mud. Together, Brendan and Isabella become lost in this game of hide-and-seek. She learnt how to hunt from her father but now it's her instructing an adult. She feels special; Brendan is an eager student. She tells him he must stay downwind of the animal. Deer have a highly refined sense of smell. She berates him for not keeping his head low enough. What if the animal sees them? She'll run. Brendan has streaks of mud on his cheeks, his chest and knees, his hands, his fingernails.

'You're nothing but mud,' says Isabella.

'So are you,' says Brendan. They giggle together and Isabella feels drawn towards him once again. Maybe before she surprised him when she tried to kiss him and he didn't know how to kiss her back; or maybe she didn't do it right; she must leave him to take the lead, not be so forward, so demanding. When she looks back she sees that Sasha has not followed them. Arms folded, sulky, she sits with her back against the stream's bank.

'Leave her,' says Brendan. 'You're with me, Isabella?'

'Yes,' she whispers. 'I'm with you.'

Still on their bellies, they slide through the undergrowth. The deer is eating. They are close enough. Brendan loads his gun, clicks the barrel into place as quietly as possible in order not to startle the deer. He brings the sight up to his eye, guides it across the body of the animal. Head or heart. He'll go head. The cross moves to the soft white fur of her chest, then up. He has her head in his sight, just between the ears. They twitch forward and back as he tries to settle on the right target.

'She's sensed something,' he whispers. 'I need to go or I'll lose her.' His fingers squeeze the trigger. A shot rings out. The deer falls. She whimpers and struggles.

'You missed,' says Isabella.

She takes the gun from Brendan, her hand dips into his pocket for another round. She reloads the gun as quickly as she can. A small amount of blood trickles from the deer's head as it lies there helpless, unable to move and unable to die – Isabella can't bear to see this suffering. Through the gun's sight, she scans down from the animal's head, down her neck. She remembers her lessons with her father: between the front legs, then up and left. Never shoot a deer in the head, because the target is too small; you're likely to miss. The circle of the gun's sight hovers over the deer's heart, cream-coloured fur pulsating frantically. Isabella squeezes the trigger. A crack. The deer slumps. Sasha begins to cry. Brendan and Isabella stand up, rush towards its body.

'We did it,' says Brendan, putting his arm around Isabella to pull her in for a hug. 'We did it. You did it.' Brendan drops down to touch her. His hand runs along the soft fur down her throat and her chest. He encourages Isabella to do the same. Still warm. Isabella has a feeling of mastery, of conquest, of power; and she likes that feeling. Brendan slices the deer open along the seam of her belly using the hunting knife. Guts spill out on to the grass, steam rising from them. They wobble like grey jelly. Next, Brendan sweeps his hands around her insides to clear out any remains. Then, he ties the rope around the muzzle of the deer, pulling it over and under, then around its neck. Holding one end of the rope, he pulls. It's heavy work but slowly, carefully, he manages to drag the deer, flopping down the hill behind him.

At the shrine, he drops the rope, collapses on to the earth beside his kill, panting from all the effort. The deer's pelt is wet; sand sticks to her. Head muddied, her belly is bloodied and gaping. Brendan slices around the neck to begin to tease the pelt away from the flesh. Removing the skin is like removing a sweater. He tugs at it until the skin underneath is visible. Grey and shiny, surgical, with little droplets of blood sticking to it. Sasha is in tears.

'It's just a deer,' snaps Isabella.

'There are plenty more,' replies Brendan. 'And they're pests.'

'As if you would know,' mutters Sasha.

When the animal is skinned, Brendan lays it on a plastic

218

sheet. Using the serrated edge of the hunting knife, he saws off each leg. Next, he removes the saddle, using swipes of the smaller knife. He lines up the meat, then gets on with the fire.

After they've eaten – even Sasha let Brendan shave off little pieces of the cooked meat with a knife to feed her, but only because she was starving and there was nothing else – the light is already fading. Brendan makes up the beds inside the shrine, tells them it's time for him to go.

'I thought you would stay too?' says Isabella.

'This is your journey,' says Brendan, and he leaves.

Isabella feel confused but doesn't tell her sister. Instead, she huddles beside her on the mattress. They wrap themselves in the duvets, hope the candles will last. Sasha has her drawing pad propped up on her knees, sketching the sea. For foaming crests of waves, she leaves the page blank. The rest of the water, she shades heavily in dark blue, sometimes black. In the distance, on the horizon, she sketches in a rowing boat thrashing about the waves.

'Put us in it!' says Isabella.

Using black, Sasha draws in the two girls, scribbles in red for their clothes.

'We're very far out to sea,' says Isabella. 'And you've forgotten the oars.'

'We couldn't be closer in. I'd already coloured in everything else. The horizon was the only bit available.'

So Isabella takes another piece of paper, draws an identical scene. Then she adds in the fin of a shark, a capsized boat, two girls in the water – damsels in distress, their arms in the air, mouths perfect circles of shock – with little word bubbles. *Help!!!!!* she writes. Then in the other girl's speech bubble: *No, don't help. We're fine.*

'Stupid drawing,' says Isabella, scrunching it up.

They drop the pencils, put the paper away, lie back on the mattress beside each other. A candle dies. Isabella replaces it with one from the bag of spares. They feel cold, bewildered. This must be serving a purpose, though, otherwise Brendan wouldn't have left them here. The sea washes up against the shore. They pile two more duvets on top of themselves, then lie underneath them, arms around each other, still wearing woolly hats and sweaters. When it's time to sleep, Sasha blows out the candles, then picks her way through the dark, jumps straight back under the covers, shivering, shuffling up close to Isabella.

They can't sleep. They feel wasted, strung out by the cold. Their bones ache. Noises keep them awake. They don't have a torch, or any matches. Sasha wants to go inside; so does Isabella. Stupid Brendan. What was he thinking, forcing them down here like this? Enough! Through the dark, Isabella pats around the edge of the shrine, finds the door, pushes it. Nothing. She pushes harder. Still, it won't open. She leans all of her body against it, feet pressing into the floor, shoulder hard against it, rams. Still, it doesn't move.

'He's locked us in. He's chained the door.' She kicks it, bangs with her fists, yells, screams, beats the door, until she only has the strength to slump to the floor, out of breath.

All night, it rains. Water thrashes the roof, dribbles in through cracks in the planks, seeps into their mattresses. They move their beds away from the wall in the hope of keeping them dry, but it doesn't work. Sitting up, damp and miserable, they resolve to stay awake all night, but then the next thing they know, they open their eyes to hear the chain rattling. The door is open. Brendan is standing in front of them. Isabella sneezes.

'Well done, girls! You survived the night!'

'Why did you lock us in?' says Isabella.

'To keep you safe,' Brendan replies.

'We were scared,' Sasha tells him.

'I never said any of this was going to be easy,' replies Brendan.

He already has a fire going, has made hot chocolate, which he pours into tin mugs for the girls. Wrapped in their sleeping bags, they drink it while Brendan tinkers with the boat. 'We're going to row north to Fior together. Very remote. Very beautiful. It's going to be wonderful. Very cleansing and healing. For all three of us.'

The girls are angry. They don't want to speak to him, so they wander off together, nudging shells out of the sand with their toes. Tangles of kelp stalks litter the beach, dumped on to the shore by the violence of the previous night's weather. Isabella finds a long, curled shell lined with mother-of-pearl. She shows it to Sasha, who holds it up to the sunlight to admire its sparkle. Isabella grabs it back, slips it into her pocket.

'But before we go, Sasha,' says Brendan, laying out blankets inside the shrine. 'I realise you haven't yet been rebirthed. It's your turn.'

'I don't want to,' replies Sasha.

'You won't get better if you don't do the work.'

Inside the shrine, a hand on each of her shoulders, he coaxes Sasha to lie down. Her eyes search out Isabella. She's scared, but she lets Brendan push her on to the mattress anyway. Arms stiff by her side, she lies tense with apprehension. Brendan covers her, holding the blankets firmly in place until she is unable to move at all. It's hot, difficult to breathe. Her eyes are open. Would he really do something to hurt her? Her heart hammers. The blanket scratches at her nose, but she can't free her arms to remedy it. She begins struggling, but the blanket is so tight she can't get out. Brendan's weight is trapping her, his determination. His deep voice commands her to fight. 'Come on, you little wimp. Fight. Live. You want to be alive, don't you?'

But she doesn't. She wants to cry. She wants him to stop. She wants to be with David, watching the waves break, sketching the birds. She has no energy. She can't do this. His knee is hurting her wrist. She needs to free a leg to kick him away, but she can't. And now she can't breathe, either, but she'll have to fight, because she has no choice other than to wrestle the weight of him away or she'll die.

Would he let her die? Harder and harder, she tries. She needs help, she can't breathe, she's hot, tired, she can't do this any more. Isabella tells Brendan to stop. He refuses. Discomfort is part of the process. She must fight her way out, just as a baby would. She must shed off her past, be reborn, be new. No longer an orphan, but a child of nature, of the gods, of this new world.

'You're mad,' Isabella says. She tries to push Brendan away.

'I can't breathe,' yelps Sasha.

'Get off her,' Isabella yells.

Still, Brendan carries on. Sasha vomits. Isabella begins hitting him, punching at his shoulders, at his back, all the time begging for him to stop.

'Resistance is part of the process. When she succumbs, she'll be cured.'

Cured of what? Isabella wonders.

But then the blanket flies up. Sasha is free. Sweating, angry, fighting back tears, wiping her mouth on her sleeve, gulping for breath. She pushes Brendan away, stumbles towards the door for air.

Outside, with barely any time to recover, Brendan orders them into the boat.

'I don't want to,' says Sasha.

'This is the nice bit,' he says. 'The homecoming. The moment of clarity, of beauty, of overcoming. We're all on this journey together.'

Shaking, upset, Sasha does as she's told and gets into the

223

boat. Sitting alongside her sister, she keeps quiet as Brendan starts rowing. At their feet slumps a brown canvas rucksack. Brendan explains that it contains several half-litre bottles of water, chocolate bars, cheese sandwiches wrapped in foil, a flask filled with instant soup to drink once the cold hits.

'Once the cold hits?' says Isabella.

'Never mind,' says Brendan. He sweats as he tugs at the oars, pulling them far out to sea until Fior appears as a speck on the horizon. Without speaking, Brendan puts down his oars. They drift. Brendan takes a small bucket, trails it through the water. He asks Sasha to lie back on the bench. She's too scared to resist. He wants her to lie on her back, dangle her head over the water. The edge of the boat digs into her neck. It hurts, but she doesn't complain. She lies very still, trying not to shake or to cry. She squeezes her eyes shut.

Brendan picks up the bucket. 'Don't move,' he says. Very gently, he pours the water over her forehead, letting it run out through her hair and back into the water. He mutters some words. She shakes with the cold. Rebirth, transformation, God's child. She can't make out everything he's saying. Soon he will stop, all this will be over. He seems skittish, agitated – not as controlled as she's used to – so when she sits up, Sasha thanks him in the hope it will placate him. With wet hair, her skull feels frozen, her teeth begin to chatter. Isabella reaches for her sister's hand. Sasha grips it. Next, it's Isabella's turn. He pours the water over her head, mutters the same mad words. When it's over, she sits beside her sister. Shivering and scared, unsure what Brendan will do next.

Brendan bends to kiss first Sasha, then Isabella. 'Thank you,' he says. 'Thank you for coming on this journey with me.' Carefully, he treads his way across the boat. The girls grip the sides, grip each other. The boat tips and rocks.

Opposite them, Brendan is standing on the seat. The breeze catches his hair, making him look wilder, madder. He holds his arms out to the sides. Like this, in the shape of a cross, he towers above them.

'Girls, now you must find your own path. Your time has come. Your own rite of passage. Your journey to adulthood. Your way out of the wilderness to return home.' Still holding his arms out, he carries on. 'And now it's time for my transformation, my own journey onwards into the unknown.'

The girls stay very still.

Brendan lets his head fall backwards. He takes deep breaths. 'God will decide what she wants to do with me,' he whispers. His toes rise from the deck, his arms move back a little. On his heels, he begins falling backwards, tumbling towards the water until he crashes down into the sea, sending up a wave around him so it looks as if the sea has gulped him down. The girls' eyes lock on to the space into which he disappeared. This is one of his tricks. Isabella has a blanket ready. He'll be struggling when he comes up.

The cold water will have brought him back to his senses. Why so mad? Before it was fun, but this isn't fun. Does he mean it as a joke? He'll put his hands on the side of the boat, they'll pull him back in, thrashing and kicking, blowing out water through his nose and he'll realise what an idiot he's been.

But there's only stillness. The sea is wickedly opaque. A glossy black shield. Three bubbles rise, popping on the surface, evaporating into the air. Gone. Isabella feels as if liquid concrete is spreading up through her limbs, hardening in her chest, her heart, her lungs, her head. She struggles to breathe. Sasha can't move. She's rooted to the spot, with no idea what to do. Her sister's eyes are wide and blank. Sasha can see on Isabella's face what she feels on her own: terror, shock, disbelief. Where are they? Miles from land, too scared to row, too scared to do anything. They just sit there, rising and falling with the boat and the waves.

In the distance, a shape bubbles up to the surface. Face down in the water, wet clothes pillow upwards. Isabella rows towards it – this is their chance – but she can't get control of the boat. Each time she thinks she is pushing towards the body, she realises she has surfed backwards, but she keeps rowing with all of her strength until finally the body is close. She hangs over the side, tries to grab his arm. The boat rocks sharply. A wave hits from the side. Brendan is right beside them now.

'Careful,' says Sasha.

Isabella can just about grab him. Laid out flat across the

boat, her sister holding her legs, she grabs hold of his trousers at the ankle and doesn't let go. The boat is knocked by another wave. It bangs into the body. Isabella tries hard to hold on to him, to pull him back on to the boat, but she can't. The body tips downwards, sinks out of sight. The surface of the water twitches.

'He's dead,' says Sasha.

'How are we ever going to row home?' says Isabella.

Grey water. Grey sky. The horizon is nothing more than a distant, blurry line between all this grey. A small wave unravels; its white foam rolls away into nothing. The endless, gentle rhythm of the sea.

Beneath them – could it be right underneath them? – the body dances with the current. Isabella can't get the image out of her head: bouncing along the seabed, sending up spurts of sand and shells, twirling in the current, carried by the little whirlpool of energy pushing it onwards. Complete freedom. Isabella wishes it was her, swallowed up by the sea, returning to the comfort of a place she knows rather than being stuck out here shivering, worrying about being punished. How could they have been so stupid?

The grey afternoon inches towards evening. Still rowing, exhausted, the girls spot a bright red helicopter heading towards them. Someone must have seen something. Are they searching for them, a couple of fugitive teenagers, or is it the missing adult playing around beneath them that they want? The helicopter turns towards the girls. Isabella pulls the oars as hard as she can. But then the helicopter turns away and, once again, there's only water. They drift. The mist thickens. They're lost. The helicopter switches on its searchlight. Its beam looks like a cylinder of glass filled with smoke.

'The fog is a punishment from God,' says Isabella. 'We'll never be found now.'

'We're lost,' replies Sasha, beginning to cry. 'And we can't see anything. And no one is looking for us.'

'Stay strong,' snaps Isabella. 'We'll be fine. This is a test and we're going to pass it.'

Isabella knows they'll be fine because this is the place they belong. Every sea otter, dolphin and gannet is a part of this world that is a part of them: each belongs to the other's history. Even though they've witnessed the sea's violence – they know that it takes what it wants without fear of retribution – they also know it won't do that to them. Sasha weeps. Isabella pulls defiantly on the oars. Her hair is misted with damp, cheeks sticky from the salt air. Sasha looks down at her cold feet. They must belong to someone else, because she is at home, sitting by the fire. Her mother has brought her a blanket and a hot chocolate, and is smoothing her forehead with a warm hand. Twilight deepens into night. Isabella pulls the oars into the boat. No point tiring herself out. The sea will do what it wants with them anyway. She rummages underneath the bench, hands a life jacket to Sasha, keeps one for herself. Together, they carefully unfold the boat cover, lay it across the damp floor to make a dry place to sit. They slide down on to it. Backs leaning against the bench, they hold on to one another and surrender. As long as there is no storm, they will gradually drift to shore, because everything washes up eventually.

geraniums, again

THE DEER SKIN HANGS ON A RAIL IN THE WOODSHED. IT'S beginning to smell. At this rate, it will end up crawling with maggots, so Anna must do something. She holds her breath to fold the skin into a neat square, which she carries at arm's length out to the garden. There, she sets it aside while she digs a hole, then carefully lays the skin within the hole, fur side up. She scrapes the soil back over it, stamps it down, to ensure a proper burial, then returns the spade to the shed. It feels like an accomplishment, a piece of mastery. She wouldn't mind doing the same to the shrine, make it disappear, along with Brendan's suitcase, his shirts and his neatly folded Y-fronts. She'd phoned his brother, a man she's never met who works for a telecoms company in New Zealand, to tell him the news. Where should she send his things?

'Throw them away,' he'd told her. How unmoved by it all he was. The brother told Anna she ought to manage things as best as she could, because there was no point in him travelling halfway across the world when they couldn't even have a funeral. They wouldn't be able to put his house on the market until they had a death certificate, so what would there be for him to do?

'What a kind man Brendan must have been,' Jerri is saying to the girls as Anna enters the kitchen to make a start on lunch.

'But a terrible shock for them,' says Anna, irritated by Jerri's insistence on keeping everything positive.

'If only he'd worn a life jacket,' Jerri replies.

'The girls were the ones who saved themselves,' Anna says.

'He wouldn't have survived those temperatures, even with a life jacket,' says David.

After lunch, Anna goes to clear out Rachel and Peter's room. Jerri didn't want to do it, so she asked Anna if she'd mind. Anna did mind, but didn't say so. In the room, the bed is still unmade, so she starts there. She pulls off the sheets, tumbles them into a messy ball, dumps them in the corner. Next, she gathers up the towels from the bathroom floor, then starts on Rachel's wardrobe.

Which bits of their lives should she save? On the dressing table: a pile of coins, old receipts, a lipstick. Inside the drawers, she gathers up socks, underwear, handkerchiefs, which she throws down alongside some old shirts and sweaters. At the back of the drawer, among Rachel's tights, she finds a photograph. A man leaning up against the trunk of a redwood tree. Young, good-looking, wearing cowboy boots. Beside him, the light dapples over an empty stretch of road. Anna tears up the photograph, flushes it down the loo. Jewellery, make-up, perfume – all the little relics she thinks the girls will enjoy – she puts in a box to take downstairs for them, but Jerri says they've gone to the shrine for one last visit before they leave.

Anna finds the girls covering photographs of Rachel and Peter in plastic sheets to protect them from the sea air. Once this is done, they nail them into the walls in careful formations. Alongside, Isabella hangs a silver necklace, Peter's watch, some red beads, until one of the shrine's walls is covered in these souvenirs. In the corner, on a small table, lies a pair of Peter's reading glasses, then candles, flowers, photographs of the four of them together. Beside it, Rachel's diving shoes, some cufflinks, gold earrings, a plant identification book, a blue dress shirt, sunglasses, a red passport. While Isabella carries on curating these objects, shifting them around, admiring them, then moving them again until she's happy, Sasha cuts strips of duct tape, which she sticks along the gaps between the planks. 'To keep the sand and the rain out,' she says. 'Otherwise all this stuff will get damaged.'

When she's finished, they arrange a small seating area with cushions and blankets. They sit, test, rearrange, move the cushions into a new place, worry and discuss, then move them back into the previous place again.

* * *

The next morning, Anna makes sure all the windows are locked. David throws dust sheets over the furniture, closes the shutters in the library, and they squeeze into the car. A sea mist leaks across the landscape. The girls hang over the backseat to watch the house disappear behind them. Jerri keeps telling them they can come back whenever they want. 'Not a thing will change, girls,' she says. 'This place will always be here. We can come every summer, if you like.'

'The cat's crying,' says Sasha. 'I don't think she likes her box. Can we take her out?' Anna agrees. The cat looks grateful as she settles into Sasha's lap, her tail swishing around as the girls stroke it.

They spend the night in York, leave just before lunch the next day. By the late afternoon, they're approaching London. The city's energy pulsates outwards; it's a magnetic force that sucks everything towards it. The cars seem glossier and sleeker, travelling faster. Within this energy, Anna feels a sense of possibility again. The city is a bestower of gifts. It chose to give to her – and it doesn't give to everybody. Anna knows she is privileged.

As they drive through the streets, pubs are expanding on to the pavements. People sit on the kerbs, flicking cigarette ash into the drains. David drops Jerri at Paddington station, then continues on home, where he helps Anna unload the car. He takes the cases to the door, leaves them on the step. For now, he'll live in a hotel. They will work out what to do with the girls once David is settled.

He hands Anna the car keys. 'You take it,' he tells her. 'I want you to have it.'

At first, it feels like an act of generosity; of protection; of masculine selflessness. He doesn't want her to suffer at all – he is the stronger one, the one who will tolerate the suffering – but as Anna takes the keys from him, puts them in the pocket of her jeans, she realises he's being practical. The permit has seven months left on it, and it won't be any use to him in his hotel in Clerkenwell. There, he'd have to keep an expensive parking meter topped up, which he'd rather not do.

They stay silent for a moment. The memories bubble up in a jumble, feelings too. Love, tenderness, hate, warmth, and a kind of viciousness – a desire to hurt him – that Anna doesn't recognise as part of her personality at all. She doesn't know what to do with all of this. Has the hatred and viciousness always been there, meticulously concealed under the shopping lists and recipes, as she lost herself within her role? He looks confused, tentative as he turns to walk away. She doesn't want to experience this new shape to her life. She didn't ask for it; but she refuses to wallow. As he walks, he turns to look back at her, to watch her enter the house. They became a habit for each other, a habit that he felt compelled to break, like smoking. Is he proud? Does he see it as a show of the strength of his will? This is all too much, so she goes inside, switches on the lights, opens the curtains, returns the cat's bed to its rightful place by the fire. During the day, Avery went in to make up the girls' beds, switch on the central heating. The girls mount the stairs, carrying their little black suitcases, to see their room.

They stand in the doorway, eyes flickering. 'Smaller than you're used to,' says Anna. 'But it's lovely and bright. There's a nice view of the garden. It won't be long until all the leaves are out.'

The girls put down their cases. Sasha sits on the bed. Isabella stands in front of the window.

'It's nice,' she says.

'I think I'd like to go to bed and read,' says Sasha.

'Good idea,' replies Anna. She shows the girls the bathroom, fetches them each a towel. Downstairs, in what's left of the light, she does a tour of the garden. There's work to do, but it's not a job for now. All she can manage is the geraniums. They're withered. She pulls them out. The stalks are mushy and brown from all the rain. They disintegrate as she touches them, leave a slimy residue on her hands.

Anna sleeps surprisingly well. The bed feels spacious. The room quiet. The next morning, Avery calls. She tells Anna she ought to go to therapy, to analyse what happened: take a cold, harsh look at her own part in it all. It'll be good for her. But Anna doesn't want to. She comes off the phone and heads out to buy an electronic label machine from the homeware shop up the road. Instead of self-examination, she'll organise her spice rack. While the girls sleep, she sits at her kitchen table, printing labels off, sticking them on to the little glass bottles. Never again will she have to guess, or rummage. They'll be there for her to see. Very simple, very straightforward. How could she possibly miss David when her drawers are this tidy? It's a liberation, in fact! She can do what she wants. As soon as she's finished the spice drawer, she starts on the top shelf of the fridge. Pickles, mustard, hot chilli sauce: all the things that David likes, thrown straight into the bin. Who needs a shrine to their former life? A rebuke feels much better.

Anna is still going when the phone rings. It's David. 'They've found Brendan,' he says. 'A fisherman spotted him on the beach.'

'And?' says Anna.

'Well, he's dead, if that's what you mean.'

'It's not what I meant,' she replies.

'He was reckless,' says David. 'Being that far out to sea in a rowing boat.'

'I'll call his brother,' says Anna.

A silence, then: 'I want to come home. I miss you. I miss everything.'

David's voice sounds plaintive, sad. It begins to work on Anna, to soften her around the edges but just in time she catches herself.

'No,' she snaps.

'I don't know what happened to me up there. I was confused. I was grieving. I lost it. I realised lying alone in a hotel, that I made a mistake. I want to come home. Please, Anna.'

All this is true, thinks Anna.

'I want everything to go back to the way it was,' says David. The sad voice again.

Anna softens once more. She feels powerless when David works on her like this. He knows the things to say, knows how to dismantle her resolve, mould her into exactly the thing he wants, like a piece of putty.

She hates him. He's alone in a hotel room. She mustn't let him do this. 'No,' she snaps again. 'Not yet, anyway. And stop calling it home.'

When the girls awake, Anna doesn't tell them that Brendan has been found. Instead, she takes them for a walk, with the news tucked away inside her. They wander through the back streets, admiring the brightly painted houses on their way, until they reach the high street. Anna buys them an ice cream each, which they eat leaning up against the outside of the shop, with the traffic rushing past. They ask her when David is coming home. Anna says she doesn't know, which they seem to accept. When they finish their ice creams, Anna texts Avery to see if she's free – she is – and the four of them agree to meet at the V&A to queue for cancellations for a new fashion exhibition. They're lucky, they get four returns, and spend the rest of the afternoon wandering the labyrinth of tiny mannequins fitted with stiff clothes. The girls enjoy it, Anna less so. The outfits look so uncomfortable.

When it's over, they walk home. Avery points out landmarks to the girls: a tiny, cobbled alleyway famous for a nineteenth-century murder; an old tobacco shop, barely changed for two centuries; a couple of locations for Hollywood movies. The girls like the stories about the movies. They want to know who the actors were. Then Isabella asks Anna to take pictures of them on her phone standing in the exact spot the actors stood. Can she send them to Tina? Anna does, and almost immediately a message comes back to congratulate them on their move to London. How are they feeling? The girls seem buoyant as they walk ahead of Anna and Avery on their journey home. Avery suggests stopping at a restaurant she knows. Would the girls like takeaway pizzas? They would, so Avery queues to order them. Then they continue their walk home, Anna carrying the boxes while Avery chatters with the girls.

When they arrive back, the house is dark and empty, which feels strange to Anna. Normally, David would be home by now, sending her little messages to ask where she'd got to, and she'd feel loved and connected, as if she was a part of something. Avery seems pleased to have the two girls around. She turns the oven on for them, insists they reheat the pizzas, even though the girls say they don't care. While they wait, Avery wants to hear about their life in Scotland. Have they known anything other than the island? Did they ever visit Tina in California? When the food is ready, Avery throws cushions on the floor in the sitting room, and they share the pizzas in front of the television.

the shrine

AT THE SHRINE, THE KITTIWAKES CIRCLE THE DAMP, BLACK branches of the trees. The fallen leaves beneath them curl up, so that each one holds within it a little pool of water. But then the winter comes, bringing snow. Life scampers into hiding. The sea is a cold sheet of pale blue. The silence is broken only by the howling of the wind, but then the ice melts and the sun dries out the shrine, making it warp. Once more, the grass is bright green. The sky shifts. A carnival of screeching emanates from the thick blanket of birds breeding on the shores. The sea boils and froths, and then autumn again. The light becomes muted. A beam comes loose, thuds to the ground. Within the gap left by the fallen beam, the dry leaves blow inside, skidding across the floor, settling into piles in the corner. Spiders make it their home, spinning their delicate threads. Then come the seagulls, flapping into the small space, but they can't get back out. They panic, splattering the ground with white mess. Salt mist blows in, leaving watermarks over the girls' photographs. The plastic protecting them begins to crackle and turn opaque, obscuring the faded images within. Rachel's diving shoes are nibbled by mice. Peter's glasses rust. The damp makes the books swell out like accordions. A storm dislodges another plank, creating an even bigger gap, allowing the wind to enter. The wind chooses its own positions for all the girls' objects. Squirrels scatter about among them, hoping for nuts; birds peck at the floor; mice leave behind their droppings; a roe and her fawn shelter from the rain. When spring returns, plants push up through the cracks in the floor, splintering the wood even more. They grow vigorously, wantonly, glossy and green and alive, until their lushness forms a glorious victory, and finally, nature has succeeded in reclaiming the shrine all for itself.

Acknowledgements

I'd like to thank the wonderful team at Tinder, particularly Imogen Taylor. Thank you for making this a better novel – and thank you also for your patience! Lizzy Kremer, my brilliant agent, was on this journey right from the start. Thank you for sticking it out!

I'm indebted to Michele Roberts who not only read early drafts but trekked across London to sit outside for socially distanced discussions on freezing cold evenings. Thank you! You helped me – and this book – enormously.

I'm grateful to Eve Wedderburn for early readings of the manuscript, tactful feedback and kind words. Thank you!

Thank you to Adam Duguid for the detailed descriptions of deer stalking because lockdown forbade me from seeing it for real. Thank you also to Jonathan Hendry for answering a steady stream of shrine building questions. Neither building nor deer stalking are skills of mine and I hope I got them right.

Thank you to artist Henry Krokatsis for sharing his

work on shrines with me and for organising my visit to his wonderful shrine, House of the Indifferent Fanatic, at Mellerstain House in the Scottish Borders. And thank you to Jane, Countess of Haddington for allowing me in to Mellerstain on a snowy Scottish day to spend time with Henry's work; and thank you also for the lovely lunch.

Thank you to Larissa and Milan Nedelkovic for letting me borrow their studio during lockdown. It gave me quiet and solitude enabling me to finish the book at a time when quiet and solitude were tricky to find.

Thank you to my dad for bringing me milk in the mornings when I was stuck in my own wilderness in the woods attempting to write and to homeschool. It's the small things that make a difference!

And of course, a big, heartfelt thank you to Nico Hameon for juggling many conflicting obligations in order to ensure that I had the time to write. It didn't go unnoticed! I didn't know how we were going to make it through lockdown but we not only survived it, we are – most importantly – still speaking to one another.

And of course thank you to Jago and Addy for being funny, bright little handfuls who never fail to take my mind off my work and remind me that the outside world still exists.

THE CABIN
A piece by Sarah Duguid
on family fracture and loss

I grew up in an old Georgian house surrounded by fields and a farm. There was a lake we could swim in, and a walled garden that provided raspberries and strawberries as well as beehives for honey. It was a privileged child-hood – materially, I was lucky – but when I was fourteen my parents divorced, bitterly, and my father found a new partner who made it clear she didn't like it when I visited. Overnight, I became unwelcome in the only home I'd ever known. Eventually, things became so fraught, we were no longer able to visit, and my dad decided he'd build a cabin in the woods at the bottom of the garden.

As a student, my Shakespeare tutor said if you stand far enough back, we humans only have a handful of stories to tell. The construction of the cabin felt like one of those stories, a primal impulse, an archetypal fable, that didn't take much standing back from to analyse. I thought of Hansel and Gretel as I watched the skeleton of timber gradually evolve into an actual building, hidden away from sight among the trees.

It took six weeks to finish – and it was beautiful. Covered in cedar shingle, it looked like a piece of land art. Yet it was a tough place to stay in for longer than a night or two, especially with a small child. The budget had been tight. The builders had worked wonders with the money they had but still, it wasn't a house. The kitchen was tiny. The shower leaked. The mice and rats were tenacious. During a cold spell, icy air would stream in through a gap underneath the bed. We'd be layered up in socks and sweaters in order to fall asleep. Also, alone in the woods at night, I was scared. During a full moon, I'd look out at the trees lit in silvery shadow and wonder who else might be out there. Did they know I was here? Did they wonder what spoils might be inside? I'd glance across at my sleeping son knowing that my dad's step-grandchildren were safely locked inside the house, enjoying the nice fires and hot meals I'd once enjoyed in there.

'You better use it,' my dad kept admonishing. 'I went to a lot of trouble to build that. She wasn't at all happy with me for doing it.'

One time, I was staying alone in the cabin with my three-year old son when there were high winds. I was afraid of a tree falling on us. I stood with my son at dad's front door and asked to be allowed inside. He shuffled off. I heard angry whispering between him and his partner. He returned to say that I could come in, but I must sit in the other room while they ate. I refused. He shuffled off again. More angry whispering. Dad returned with the offer of a compromise: I could stay with them in the dining room while they ate, but neither me nor my son would be given any food.

I lay in my bed in the cabin that night, listening to the creak of the trees, scared that at any moment one would come down and finish us both off. What the hell was I doing? What was this building? I got stuck on the thought that I was sleeping in a shrine, a memorial to a life I'd lost and would never regain. That thought was the spark for my novel *The Wilderness*. I wanted to think about memory and loss, how we sometimes need the things we lose to leave a mark, a physical mark, because memory is too capricious, too evanescent: it lets things fade. I wanted the shrine in my novel to be an empty, pointless building made from cheap, everyday materials, but nevertheless would be imbued with significance for each character; its unwieldy presence would crystallise something for them. For the two girls in *The Wilderness*, the shrine is a womb. Rather like a church, it represents the sacred maternal body, the source of creation; the loss of the maternal and the urge to return to it. Whereas for Anna, it represents an obstacle, a thing to be fought against, like her oppressive, bourgeois marriage.

Over time, despite constant pressure from dad, I visited the cabin less and less. I was also struggling with my writing. I drafted and re-drafted the novel I was working on, but couldn't get it to hang together. As one last ditch attempt, I decided to return to the cabin for the summer. If I couldn't complete it by the autumn, then that really was it.

By this time, dad's partner had died very suddenly and unexpectedly. Without the complexities of exile, I began to enjoy the space, to revel in the calmness. I loved waking in the middle of the night and watching muntjac idling in trees, bathed in monochromatic moonlight. I went to bed at the same time as the children, then woke at five, took a walk through the woods before settling down to write. And the writing came, it began to flow, feelings returned, the ideas came together. Later, dad trundled down in his Land Rover to deliver fresh milk from the farm and we'd have a coffee together.

The novel was soon finished but then, dad was diagnosed with terminal cancer. It was aggressive, he didn't have long to live. The Covid rules had led to a shortage of carers. We were on a list for support, but in the meantime, had only limited help. Dad wanted to die at home so, in the end, I said I'd care for him in order to avoid a hospice.

It was a tough few months, tougher than I could ever have foreseen. His funeral felt like the final, horrible practicality after three months of nothing other than horrible practicalities. At the burial, my imagination didn't leap towards the ethereal. I didn't see signs from God, no circling birds or magical changes in the light. I saw a flat, overcast day, a wooden box in a hole. I knew every inch of the frail body within that box because I'd washed it, many times. I examined the way the earth changed as the hole got deeper. I couldn't wait for it all to be over. I didn't even want to go to the wake. Instead, I lay on a pew in the empty church, while my husband dismantled all the wires and cameras he'd set up for the Zoom broadcast.

Images of my father's suffering began to haunt me, sometimes so vividly they stopped me in my tracks. I couldn't bear to visit his grave because I didn't want the feelings it evoked. But in the cabin, I felt at peace. Again, it became a shrine, of sorts. I'd remember the sight of him delivering milk. I'd think about the time we had Christmas Eve dinner at a wobbly trestle table and he drank so much crème de menthe he couldn't walk home. It was in that quiet, special place, listening to the wind rustle through the trees that I felt as if I was surrounded by the good parts of him, the kindness, the fatherliness, and I forgot the rest: the suffering, the hole in the ground, how I felt about the fact that I ever had to sleep in a cabin at all.